Betteken's REFUGE

© 2015 by TGS International, a wholly owned subsidiary of Christian Aid Ministries, Berlin, Ohio.

All rights reserved. No part of this book may be used, reproduced, or stored in any retrieval system, in any form or by any means, electronic or mechanical, without written permission from the publisher except for brief quotations embodied in critical articles and reviews.

ISBN: 978-1-941213-70-4
Cover and text layout design: Kristi Yoder
Cover art: Shirley Myers, based on sketch by Hannah Lehigh
Illustrations throughout layout: Hannah Lehigh

Printed in the USA

Published by:
TGS International
P.O. Box 355
Berlin, Ohio 44610 USA
Phone: 330.893.4828
Fax: 330.893.2305
www.tgsinternational.com

TGS001046

Betteken's
REFUGE

Maeyken Wens' story through
the eyes of her daughter

Diane Yoder

The LORD is my light and my salvation; whom shall I fear? The LORD is the strength of my life; of whom shall I be afraid? Psalm 27:1

TABLE OF CONTENTS

1. Betteken's World 7
2. A Walk in the City 19
3. The Cost 27
4. "I Must Go" 35
5. Johannes the Printer 41
6. The Stranger's Message 51
7. Father's Return 61
8. Whom Shall I Fear? 69
9. Adriaen's Questions 77
10. Why Pray? 83
11. A Trip to Rotterdam 91
12. "You Must Forgive" 101
13. Janneken's Baby 107
14. The Trial 117
15. Memorial in the Ashes 123
16. Father's Decision 129
    Appendix 135
    Author's Postscript 137
    Dutch Pronunciation Key 139
    About the Author 140

CHAPTER ONE

Betteken's World

*L*aughter drifted over a frozen canal in Antwerp, a city in the Spanish Netherlands. Crouched on the bank where she was tying the leather straps of her skates together, Betteken[1] Wens could watch the figures of her friends sweeping over the ice. Metal skate blades, curving up in front of their toes, flashed in the sunlight.

"Come on, Betteken," her friend Elizabeth called. "If you hurry, you can race with us before we all go home."

"I'm coming!" Standing up, Betteken quickly skated over to the group. "Where are we racing?"

"Pieter said that the first one to get to the other side of the canal wins," explained Elizabeth. "Let's go!"

"Are you sure it's safe?" asked Betteken as the girls started off to join the others. "It's a little warmer today. What if the ice is starting to melt?"

"Spring isn't here yet, you know. It is only February, and

---

[1] See Dutch Pronunciation Key on page 139.

the ice is still thick. Nothing to worry about!" Elizabeth laughed and quickened her pace, pulling ahead of Betteken.

Betteken glanced once more at the ice before pushing away her doubt. She followed her friend to where the others were lining up. The air was cold, but the sun shone bright and warm. She turned her face toward the sun and laughed aloud. It felt good to be alive on such a beautiful day.

Pieter stood before them, one arm raised. "One, two, three, go!" he shouted. Betteken's feet fairly flew across the ice. The cold air stung her cheeks, and her long dress fluttered in the wind. Glancing back, she saw Elizabeth skating up behind her. She willed herself to skate faster.

The next moment she heard a terrifying *crack!* Elizabeth screamed. Betteken pulled up sharply and whirled around just in time to see her friend plunge through the ice into the water.

In a flash, someone had grabbed Betteken's hand and was pulling her away. "Stay back," her brother Adriaen commanded. "I'll try to help her, but you must do exactly what I say. Lie down behind me and hold my feet. We don't want our weight to be all at one place, because we might break through the ice." Turning to the others who were milling confusedly about, he called, "The rest of you lie down on the ice and form a chain. Hold on to each other!"

As Adriaen dropped to his stomach on the ice, Betteken lay down to grasp his feet. Behind her, someone else took her own feet. Betteken kept her eyes on Adriaen as he scooted to where Elizabeth was just bobbing up to the surface of the water. "Elizabeth!" he called. "Take my hand!"

Elizabeth sputtered, tossing her head so that drops of water flew everywhere. She reached for Adriaen's hand, terror in her eyes. She missed and slid back under. Adriaen scooted closer to the opening, and Betteken's knuckles turned white as she held onto his feet with all her strength. Elizabeth was bobbing to the surface again. This time she reached as far as she could and grasped Adriaen's fingers.

"Grab the side of the ice with your other hand and pull yourself up, if you can." Adriaen's voice was calm and steady. "I'll try to pull you out, but you have to help me."

Elizabeth's face was pale, but she seemed to draw courage from his words. Catching the side of the ice as Adriaen had directed, she drew herself up, allowing Adriaen to grasp her shoulders. As he slowly pulled her onto the ice, the human chain behind Betteken scooted back, drawing them out of the danger zone.

Cheers filled the air as they reached the other side of the canal, but Elizabeth fell stiffly against Adriaen. The cheers died away when she began coughing up water, her lips turning blue. Adriaen spoke quickly. "We need to take Elizabeth home right away. Pieter, will you help me lift her onto my sleigh?"

In minutes, Adriaen and Betteken had left the others behind and were hurrying through the city streets to reach Elizabeth's home. Betteken watched the shivering girl with concern. Her friend had never been strong. Would she be all right?

Voices drifted out the open door of the tailor's shop at the corner ahead of them, where Elizabeth's grandfather worked. Her mother made fabric for his business, and the family lived upstairs above the shop. When Adriaen stopped the sled beside the curb, the elderly man was standing in the doorway peering at the small entourage. "What is the matter?" he rasped, bushy eyebrows drawing together.

"We must get Elizabeth near the fire as soon as possible, sir," Adriaen said quickly. "She fell through the ice while we were skating. Is her mother here?"

"Bring her into my shop." Elizabeth's grandfather opened the door wider and turned, calling up the stairs. "Elizabeth is home, and we need help!"

Elizabeth's mother entered the shop just as her daughter was being carried in. "Why, Elizabeth, you're soaked to the skin!" she exclaimed. "Here, bring her into this room. What happened?"

"We were skating on the ice, Mama," Elizabeth answered weakly. "I fell through."

The color drained from her mother's face. "Couldn't you see that the ice was melting?"

"We thought it would still be all right." Adriaen met her gaze. "I'm very sorry, Mrs. Wils."

Mrs. Wils glanced again at her daughter and smiled. "What a relief that she's safe! Betteken, will you get some heavy blankets from that closet to wrap her in?"

When Betteken returned with the blankets, Elizabeth was sitting in a chair by the fire. Though she had changed into dry clothes, she was still shivering. "Elizabeth, are you all right?"

"Mama is heating a cup of milk for me," Elizabeth replied through chattering teeth. "I should warm up then."

"We need to go, Betteken," Adriaen said softly. "I hope you feel better soon, Elizabeth."

Elizabeth managed a smile. "Thank you for helping me get out of the water, Adriaen."

"I'm so glad you were there to help my daughter," her mother added. "Come back again sometime."

Betteken squeezed Elizabeth's hand. "I'll try to come tomorrow," she promised. "Goodbye."

"Come again soon," Elizabeth's grandfather called with a broad smile as Betteken and Adriaen passed through his shop. "Anyone who saves my granddaughter's life is welcome here!"

Adriaen smiled back. "Thank you, sir. Here, Betteken, climb into the sleigh and I'll pull you home."

Betteken waved to Elizabeth's grandfather as she seated herself in the sleigh. In a moment they were skimming away, heading down the main street. Snow-roofed buildings rose tall on either side while people picked their way through the icy streets. In the distance, church bells began to ring. As they rounded a corner, Betteken saw the priest standing in the doorway of the stately cathedral.

"Do you think Father Wils saw what happened to Elizabeth?" she asked Adriaen. "The canal is just across the street."

"It's possible that he saw." Adriaen followed her gaze. The priest was turning to go back inside, his black robes rustling.

"Even though he is Elizabeth's uncle, she's a little scared of him," Betteken remarked.

Adriaen grinned. "It's those dark eyes and hair, along with the black robes, that make him look forbidding." He pulled the sleigh into their home street. The sun was setting now, its rays glancing off the stone house near the city gates. Jumping off the sled, Betteken hurried to the door.

"Mama," she called, bursting inside. "I'm sorry we're so late, but we had to take Elizabeth home."

"What was wrong with Elizabeth?" Maeyken Wens straightened from the hearth where flames danced merrily under a kettle of simmering stew. Behind her, three-year-old Hans dashed into the kitchen, waving a scopperel[2] in the air. "Betteken!" he shouted. "See what I have!"

She scooped him up into her arms. "It's pretty," she said.

"We were skating on the ice," she said, glancing at her mother over Hans's blond curls. "Elizabeth fell through, and—"

"She fell through?" Maeyken gasped.

"Adriaen helped her out," Betteken explained. "We took her home then. She was warming up by the fire when we left."

"I hope she'll be all right. This is a good reminder to be careful whenever you go on the ice," Maeyken stated. She filled a pewter pitcher with cider and handed it to Betteken. "Fill the cups on the table, please. Father is home now, and the meal will soon be ready."

Betteken could hear her father and Adriaen washing up in the entryway. Quickly setting Hans down, she took the pitcher and hurried to the table.

"Didn't you check the ice carefully to see if it was safe?" she heard her father asking.

"Not really. I was skating with my friends," explained Adriaen as they came through the door. "Then some of the girls came along too."

---
[2] A sort of pinwheel or whirligig.

"Elizabeth always loved to skate," Betteken said. "Do you think she'll be scared of ice after this?"

"She'll probably be out there again with you in no time." Mattheus Wens smiled at his daughter and turned to his wife, who was bringing a large bowl of stew to the table. "That smells wonderful, dear."

Maeyken smiled back at him. "As soon as you're seated, we're ready to eat."

Betteken felt a warm glow filling her heart as she sat down on the bench beside Adriaen. The flickering flames in the hearth cast long shadows over the kitchen, making it feel cozy. She loved this evening hour when her family was all together.

"Let's pray," her father said. He bowed his head and the rest of the family followed suit, thanking God silently for their food.

Just as they lifted their heads, a knock sounded on the door. Without waiting to be greeted, the visitor entered, bringing in a rush of cold air. Calmly Mattheus rose from his chair. "Can I help you?"

"My brother is dying, Mattheus." The young man's face was stricken, his eyes filled with fear. "He's asking for you to come pray with him."

"I will come." Mattheus picked up his hat and glanced at his wife. "It may be late before I get back, Maeyken."

"We can't turn away someone in need," she answered softly. "We'll be fine here."

As the door closed behind her father and the young man,

Betteken stared at her plate, her appetite suddenly gone. "Is it safe for Father to go out there?" she asked abruptly. "He's in more danger than the rest of us because he's a church leader. What if he gets arrested tonight?"

"Father may be in danger, but he isn't afraid." Her mother's blue eyes were kind as they met hers. "He's doing what God has called him to do."

Adriaen leaned forward slightly. "We miss him here with us, though. This is the third night in a row he's been gone to pray with someone or help somebody."

"I know. But think about what he is doing to help other people," Maeyken reminded her son. "Have you thought about how we can help his ministry? Father says that when we pray for him here at home, it gives him strength."

They didn't speak of it again. But after the dishes were washed and she was climbing the stairs to her room, Betteken's earlier question still weighed heavy on her heart.

Pausing at her door, she glanced back at Adriaen. "Do you think Father will get home safely tonight?"

Adriaen was honest with his answer. "I hope so. He always has before."

"I know. But every time he's gone, I worry about him."

"Remember that he's doing what God wants him to do," Adriaen said simply, his eyes glowing in the dim light of the candle Betteken was holding.

She closed her door and set the candle on the small block stool next to her bed. Taking off the linen cap around her head, she uncoiled her braid and picked up her brush. As she pulled it absently through her wavy blond hair, she stepped to the window and opened one shutter just a bit. Dark figures moved along the streets below, visible only because of the moonlight. Though she'd never been out on the streets at this hour, she knew the city was not safe at night.

Betteken shivered a little, closed the shutter, and drew the shades. Pulling on her nightclothes, she knelt beside her bed. "Dear God," she whispered into the darkness. "Please keep Father safe tonight. Help him to show the dying man your love. And please don't let the authorities find him. We all love him so much!"

She added a silent prayer for Elizabeth before getting up and blowing out the candle. She could hear Mama singing downstairs as she put Hans to sleep. Her sweet voice was comforting, and Betteken cracked her door open so she could hear better.

> In the world, ye saints, you'll be defamed,
> Let this be cause for pious glee;
> Christ Jesus too was much distained;
> Whereby He wrought to set us free;
> He took away of sin the bill
> Held by the foe. Now if you will
> You too may enter heaven still.[3]

Betteken had heard this song before at the Dutch Anabaptists' secret meetings. The year was 1573 now, and

---

[3] From *The Complete Writings of Menno Simons*. © 1956 Mennonite Publishing House, Scottdale, Pa. Used by permission.

people all over the Low Countries were following the teachings of men who had searched the Bible and found a way they believed God wanted His people to live. Her own father was a minister at the church here in the city of Antwerp.

Most of the Low Countries were controlled by the king of Spain. When the citizens had asked for their independence, the king refused. Instead, he raised taxes and decreed that all the people must claim membership with the state church. Seven years earlier when the Dutchmen revolted against the iron hand of the Spaniards, war had broken out.[4]

The Dutch Anabaptists refused to join the state church or take part in the political uprisings. Caught in the middle of the religious and political unrest, they lived day and night with the threat of capture hanging over them. Now, Mama's song brought comfort to Betteken's heart as she stood by the door, wondering when her father would come home. She listened to the next verse.

> If you in fires are tested, tried,
> Begin to walk life's narrow way,
> Then let God's praise be magnified,
> Stand firm on all He has to say;
> If you stand strong and constant then,
> Confess His Word in the sight of men,
> With joy He extends the diadem![5]

---

[4] The Dutch Revolt against Spain began in 1566 and went on for years.
[5] From *The Complete Writings of Menno Simons*. © 1956 Mennonite Publishing House, Scottdale, Pa. Used by permission.

CHAPTER TWO

A Walk in the City

Betteken hurried down the street, balancing a basket on her shoulder. Her mother had sent her to pick up an order of wool from Elizabeth's mother so that she could also visit her friend while she was there. Betteken had to hurry, though, because they were planning to have a secret meeting at their house later that evening.

"Betteken, wait!"

Betteken turned, and a smile lit her eyes when she saw her friend Maritgen coming toward her. "Where are you going?" Maritgen asked.

"To visit Elizabeth. Would you like to come with me?"

"I'd love to," Maritgen said instantly.

"I'm worried about her," Betteken admitted. "She got so cold the other day." She led the way down the narrow street. "Why, there's Father Wils," she exclaimed, looking ahead. "He just went into the shop. I wonder if he's going to visit Elizabeth too."

Maritgen slowed down a little. "He scares me," she

confided. "He always peers down at me so suspiciously."

"Elizabeth says she's a little scared of him too," Betteken said. "I'm just glad you're with me. Come on, let's go inside."

"Well, well," Elizabeth's grandfather exclaimed as the two girls stepped inside. "If it isn't Betteken, coming back to visit us! And you brought a friend with you today?" He smiled at them as he rose from his chair.

"We're here to visit Elizabeth, sir," said Maritgen politely.

The smile broadened on the wizened old face. Opening the door, he called to his daughter, "Maeyken! We have visitors!"

Betteken smiled to herself. She enjoyed the fact that her mother and Elizabeth's mother shared the same name.

"Betteken!" Maeyken Wils appeared in the doorway, smiling. "And Maritgen is here too. Come in!"

Elizabeth was sitting near the fire, wrapped in a heavy woolen blanket. "It's so good to see you girls," she said, her eyes lighting up. "Sitting here all day makes for a long day."

"She's developed a bad cough and sore throat," her mother explained. She tucked the blanket more securely around Elizabeth's shoulders. "With it being so cold outside, I didn't want her to go out."

"I hope you get well soon," Maritgen said.

Elizabeth started to answer but then turned away, bending nearly double with the coughing fit that racked her thin frame. The girls stepped back.

"She's been coughing like this ever since she fell through the ice," Mrs. Wils said with a frown. "If she keeps on, I'll have to ask the doctor to come."

"I told you, Mama." Elizabeth slumped back weakly in her chair. "I'm sure it's nothing to worry about. Just a slight cough."

"It's more than just a slight cough, child. Here, take some more of this boiled honey and water." Her mother handed her a small cup. "I'll leave you girls alone now."

"Maeyken?" The door opened, and Elizabeth's uncle

stepped into the room. "I thought I heard Elizabeth coughing in here. Is she all right?"

Up close, the priest looked even more forbidding than he had from the street. His long robes seemed as solemn as his face. Betteken wondered if the corners of his mouth ever turned upward. Now he bent down to look Elizabeth in the eye. "How are you feeling?"

She smiled bravely. "Not very well. But I'll probably feel better soon."

"I hope so." Much to Betteken's surprise, he smiled. "I'm glad you have friends to come and visit you."

Betteken was glad when he left the room again. She didn't want to think about what would happen if someone like the priest found out that she was the daughter of an Anabaptist minister. She reached out to squeeze Elizabeth's hand. "I hope you'll feel better soon, Elizabeth."

"Thanks." Elizabeth tilted her head to look at Betteken. "I'm glad you girls came to visit me today."

"We'll try to come again before long."

The girls said their goodbyes and left. People thronged the streets, filling the air with chatter and laughter. Wealthy ladies hurried by, sporting cloaks with fur sleeves. "How do you think it would be to own such beautiful clothes?" Betteken wondered aloud.

Maritgen laughed. "I'd feel like a queen! But I doubt that will ever happen. Well, here's where I turn. I'll see you later!"

Betteken waved and walked on, heading down her home street. She passed the site where her father was laying freestone for a new blacksmith shop. Adriaen was there too; he was planning to be a mason someday, like their father. As she drew near, Mattheus looked up and saw his daughter. "What brings you here, Betty?"

Betteken smiled. "I went to visit Elizabeth."

"How is she doing?" asked Adriaen, stepping down from his ladder.

"She has a cough and sore throat, but her mother is giving her boiled honey and water to drink. She said that if Elizabeth doesn't get better soon, she'll ask the doctor to come." Betteken glanced down the street. In the distance she could see the cathedral, and a tingle snaked up her spine. "I should go. How soon will you come home tonight, Father?"

"No later than usual. Why?"

She wanted to tell him that she was afraid of what the priest might do if he ever found out that her father was an Anabaptist minister. But she couldn't mention it here in public. Stepping back, she gave a little wave. "I just wondered. I'll see you later."

She walked slowly along the street, gazing toward the cathedral. Father Wils was a Catholic priest, but Betteken knew there were other kinds of beliefs in the Low Countries too. Only last year in Paris, France, about three thousand people from a religious group called Protestants had been put to death in one day.[1] Betteken hoped that would never happen to her father's church here in Antwerp.

She was nearing the Scheldt River now. Ships and

---
[1] St. Bartholomew's Day Massacre, 1572.

steamboats were sailing in toward the port. Merchants and traders from many corners of Europe came to Antwerp with their goods.[2] Betteken loved to dream of sailing far away on one of those big ships and seeing more of the world. But with the war going on, it was dangerous to go anywhere right now.

Now wasn't the time to linger here and think about that, though. Mama would soon be wondering where she was if she didn't come home. Betteken turned away from the river and hurried on, dodging to the side of the street as a horse-drawn carriage clattered by. From where he sat in the high seat, Father Wils didn't seem to notice her at all.

Betteken clutched her basket a little tighter and slowly started walking again.

. . . .

"Betteken! She's here, she's here!"

Betteken laughed as Hans raced up to her and caught her hand. "Who's here?" she asked, although she felt sure she knew.

"Aunt 'Etha," explained Hans, his eyes shining. "She gave me a wide on her knee!"

"A what? Oh, you mean a 'ride.'" Betteken grinned to herself and let Hans pull her through the open door.

Aunt Margretha was standing at the counter, cutting a parsnip into thin slices for salad. She turned and smiled. "Hi, Betteken. Hans was telling me about how you went to the market today. I think he wished he could have gone with you."

---

[2] Antwerp was the richest city in Europe at this time.

Betteken set her basket on the table. "He wouldn't have been able to keep up. It's a long walk, and I went to visit Elizabeth too."

Her aunt sobered. "I heard that she fell through the ice. How is she doing?"

"She's on the mend, but her cough sounds bad. Her mother said that if she doesn't get better, she'll send for the doctor." Betteken watched her aunt for a moment. Margretha was Mama's youngest sister, and she often came to help with housework. She was unmarried and had just turned twenty years old last month. Her sparkling dark eyes filled with laughter now as she glanced at Betteken.

"I'm sure that having you girls visit her is as good as any tonic for Elizabeth."

"Elizabeth's uncle—you know, Father Wils—was there too." Betteken hesitated. "I hope he never finds out who I am."

"You must be very careful," her mother said, coming into the kitchen. "It's dangerous to tell anyone who you are and where you live."

Betteken nodded and changed the subject, not wanting to think about it anymore. "What shall I do first?"

"Sweep the kitchen floor, please. After that you can help us with the meal." Mama handed her the broom.

"It's going to be really cold tonight," said Aunt Margretha.

Betteken knew she was thinking of the secret meeting they would hold in their house later that evening. She glanced toward her mother.

"Our visitors will need to dress warmly," Maeyken said. "It looks as though it could start snowing tonight." She seemed to hesitate. "Lately we've been concerned . . ." Her voice trailed off.

Betteken looked up. What did Mama mean by that? But she was already talking about something else. "I'll set the table for supper. As soon as Father and Adriaen come home, we'll eat."

Betteken turned back to her sweeping, but her mother's words niggled at her mind. *Lately we've been concerned . . .*

She shivered, as though the words had blown a cold wind into the room.

CHAPTER THREE

The Cost

"Are you truly sorry for all your sins, and are you willing to renounce Satan and the world?"

Betteken's father spoke quietly to the young man kneeling before him at the front of the room. From where she watched at the window, Betteken could hear Hans van Munstdorp answer clearly. "I am."

Betteken watched the young man closely as Father asked the last question. "Do you promise by the grace of God to submit yourself to Christ, and faithfully serve Him until death?"

There was a quiet glow in Hans's eyes when he answered, "I do."

Until death. Betteken shivered at the thought. Earlier that evening, dark figures had walked the streets to their home in small groups, after which they gathered in the parlor. "I don't think we were followed," one man had said quietly as he entered. Still, everyone was tense. Outside the wind was howling, driving snow against the stone house in blinding

27

white sheets. The house itself was dark, and only the room where they were gathered was lit by candles.

At the front of the room, Betteken's father took a dipper from the ledge above the hearth, and filled it with water. The aging minister Jan de Metser joined him, cupping his hands on the young man's head. "Upon the confession of your faith, I now baptize you in the name of the Father, the Son, and the Holy Ghost," Mattheus Wens said. Water ran down over Hans's blond hair, dripping on the cold stone floor.

The ministers baptized Hans's young wife, Janneken, next. Betteken glanced at Adriaen, who stood beside her. His blue eyes were serious, and Betteken wondered what he was thinking. He knew as well as she did that the choice to serve God and be baptized could bring danger. Just thinking about it frightened her. The secret meetings they held were against the law. If the city leaders ever found them, they would capture those who didn't escape and take them to prison. She glanced toward the window. The shutters were closed, but the image of soldiers coming down the street was so vivid in her mind that she had to force her attention back to the service.

Afterward, Betteken sought out Maritgen. Her friend's family usually attended the meetings, but tonight she'd come with only her father and brother, Pieter. "The little girls were sick," Maritgen explained. "Mama stayed home with them." Her voice lowered to a whisper. "Pieter says that he wants to be baptized soon. He has been repenting of his sins and asked God to forgive him and has decided to follow Jesus. He's been different ever since."

"Different?"

"More at peace. And not as quick-tempered either."

"When a person becomes a Christian, he changes," Betteken said thoughtfully. "I hear that a lot." She glanced around at the rapidly dwindling crowd. "Did you notice that our gatherings have been smaller than usual lately?"

"It's as though people are afraid to come," Pieter observed as he and Adriaen joined them. Tall and blond, Pieter looked much like his sister. "But I did see Janneken's sister Grietge here."

"Really?" Betteken followed his gaze to the back of the room. She hadn't seen the young woman until now.

"I wonder what Grietge is thinking about all this," Adriaen said. "She knows as well as anyone how dangerous it is for Hans and Janneken to be baptized."

"It's dangerous, all right," Pieter agreed. "Felix Straten isn't happy with their decision to be rebaptized."

"Janneken's father? How do you know that?" Maritgen asked.

"I heard Father telling Mama about it." Pieter glanced again toward the back of the room. Grietge was just opening the door, ready to leave. "I wonder if the family even knows that Grietge is here."

"I doubt it," said Adriaen. "They might not even know that Hans and Janneken were baptized tonight. If her father doesn't like it . . ." His voice trailed off.

"Would he do anything to hurt them?" The very thought made Betteken shudder.

"I hope not, but I'm not sure." Adriaen's blue eyes darkened, but he said nothing more.

Pieter and Maritgen soon said goodbye and left with their family. Betteken followed Adriaen to the front of the room, where Hans and Janneken were still talking with her parents. "God has promised to never leave you or forsake you," Mattheus was saying. "You can cling to that promise and rest in Christ. In Him you have nothing to fear."

Reaching out, Hans shook Father's hand. "We're thankful for all you've done for us, Mattheus. May God bless you."

A light shone in Janneken's eyes as she stood next to her husband. Maeyken gave her a gentle hug. "Go with God," she said softly. Then Hans and Janneken were gone, slipping silently through the door.

"It's a cold walk tonight," Betteken noted as she saw the wind whipping the cloaks of their guests.

"I hope they all make it safely home." Adriaen glanced toward his father. "There used to be a lot of people who came for meetings, but not anymore. Is it just because of the cold weather? Or is there something else?"

Holding up a candle, Mattheus searched his children's faces. "The cold weather is part of it," he said slowly. "Some of the people who usually come are sick right now. But there's more."

Betteken's throat felt tight with dread. "It's because of Father Wils, isn't it?" she blurted.

Her father looked at her steadily. "I won't lie to you, Betty. The priest wants to find us, yes, but he isn't the only one.

You know that the Duke of Alba from Spain wants to get rid of everyone who opposes the state church."

Betteken looked at her mother. "Is that what you meant earlier today when you said that you're concerned?"

Maeyken nodded. "Even though we try to keep our meetings hidden, we may be found someday," she explained. "It takes courage to face the threat of capture."

Hans stirred in his mother's arms, his eyes drooping. Maeyken glanced down at him and smiled. "It's time to start getting ready for bed," she said cheerfully. "Especially this little boy. It's already past his bedtime." Hans squealed as his mother tickled his chin, and she laughed with him.

Betteken felt relief through their laughter. She turned to Adriaen as the others left the room. "Maritgen told me tonight that Pieter wants to be baptized sometime soon."

"He told me that too." Adriaen stopped there, but Betteken wanted to know more. Though she discussed a lot of things with her brother, this was a subject they largely avoided.

"Are you planning to join him?" she asked quietly.

Adriaen didn't answer right away. "I have a lot of questions, Betteken," he said finally in a hushed tone. "Like Mama said, it takes courage to face the threat of prison and death. Since Father is a minister, the authorities are searching for him. He could get in big trouble for what he's doing.

"There's a cost involved with following Christ. Felix Straten doesn't like Hans and Janneken's decision. I don't know what he'd do, but he could hurt them." His voice tightened. "I just can't understand why God allows believers to go through things like this for their faith. He's so powerful, and He could stop it."

"Are you bitter at God?" Betteken asked. She had never heard her brother talk like this before.

Adriaen hesitated. "I just have questions, that's all. If I would decide to follow Christ and be baptized, it would change my whole life."

Betteken knew that if Adriaen did make that choice, he would do it with his whole heart. That was the way he did things. While she admired him for it, she felt afraid at the same time.

A scraping sound at the window suddenly caught Betteken's attention. "Adriaen!" she whispered, grabbing his arm. "Is someone out there?"

Stepping quickly to the window, Adriaen threw the shutters open. He drew back, his face pale. "Whoever it is just ducked out of sight!"

"Did you see the face?" Betteken asked as he peered into the darkness.

Adriaen closed the shutters again. "Not really. I only caught a glimpse."

"Do you think our house is being watched?"

"I don't know, Betteken." His voice was just above a whisper. "But we must be careful."

Betteken's heart dropped. Their way of life was bound up in secrecy. If they were discovered, many lives would be in danger. She didn't like to think of their own house being watched. She wanted a secure and safe place to call home!

But the authorities were looking for the Anabaptists. If the small groups hurrying toward their house in the night had somehow been spotted, she would have to face the truth that their home could be under suspicion.

CHAPTER FOUR

"I Must Go"

The morning sun peeked through gray clouds. Opening her eyes, Betteken yawned and stretched. So much had happened during the last few days, and it felt good to simply relax.

In that moment she remembered the face Adriaen had seen through the window the night before. A cloud covered her mind. Who could it possibly have been?

A small fist pounded on the door, breaking into her reverie. "Betteken!" Hans shouted. "Mama said it's time to get up!"

With his words, Betteken's dread from the previous night melted away. No one could be gloomy for long with little Hans around. She grinned and threw back the curtains around her bedstead, springing to the floor. Shivering in the cold air, she slipped quickly into a faded blue frock and coiled her blond hair in a braid around her head. After pulling on her linen cap, she was ready to go downstairs.

Adriaen was just coming out of his room across the hall when she opened the door. He took one look at her and whistled. "Didn't you sleep at all last night?"

"Of course I did!" But she knew why he asked. Her eyes felt heavy, as though there were weights on top of them.

"Still worried about that face in the window?" Adriaen asked. "I wonder now if we weren't just imagining things. We were talking about the priest right then, and that likely made us jumpy."

In the daylight, the shadows of the night before seemed far away. "I don't even want to think about it," Betteken said suddenly. Brushing past her brother, she ran lightly down the stairs.

She found Mama in the kitchen, bending over the fire as she stirred creamy yellow custard in the iron pot. Betteken stopped beside her, and Mama looked up with a slight smile. "Will you help Hans get dressed, Betty?"

"Sure, Mama." Betteken scooped Hans into her arms and ran a hand through his blond curls. "Let's get you ready for the day!"

The kitchen was the warmest place in the house because of the fire. Betteken carried Hans to the kitchen table to comb his hair. Adriaen was sitting on the bench against the wall behind the table, wooden shoes in hand. His eyes were on his mother as she sliced a fresh loaf of bread for breakfast. She wasn't working as quickly as usual, and there was a troubled look in her eyes that Betteken hadn't noticed before.

As she combed Hans's hair and smelled the custard, Betteken watched Mama closely. Once she was sure she saw Mama wipe away a tear. She glanced toward Adriaen and then down at her brother's curls, a prickle of fear tingling her spine. What was wrong? Why didn't anyone speak?

The door opened, and her father stood in the doorway. Maeyken glanced up, and a long look passed between them. Then she smiled, and the heaviness in her face eased a little.

Scrambling down from the table, Hans raced to his father, who scooped up his son and tossed him into the air. The small boy shouted with laughter, and Mattheus laughed too. Only then did Betteken's fear melt away.

Adriaen stood up. "Father, are we going to the building site this morning, even with the fresh snow?"

Mattheus looked out the window. "Yes, I think we should at least go for a while. I'm leaving later this afternoon, so it'd be good to have as much done as possible."

"You're leaving? Where are you going?"

Their father hesitated. "I'll tell you about it while we eat."

It wasn't like him to evade a question, and some of Betteken's fear returned. She helped her mother carry the food to the table before sitting down on the bench beside Adriaen.

She ventured to ask her father about his statement after prayer was over. "Where are you going today, Father?"

"After all of you were in bed last night, we had a visitor," Mattheus began.

Startled, Betteken glanced toward Adriaen. When their eyes met, she knew that he was also remembering the face in the window.

"The man just arrived in Antwerp last night," their father

went on. "He'd been instructed to find a man named Mattheus Wens. He'll meet me later today, and we'll travel together to Ghent."

Though he hadn't said so directly, Betteken could easily read between the lines—he was going to Ghent to preach to a group of believers there.[1] Her spoon clattered to the table. "Father," she whispered. "Some people in Ghent were killed just recently."

"I know, Betty." Her father looked at her kindly. "But I must go and encourage those left behind."

Betteken couldn't answer because of the dreadful fear that was beginning to clutch her heart. Beside her, Adriaen cleared his throat. "Father, it's dangerous to go there."

"Yes, son, it is." Mattheus looked from Adriaen to Betteken, then at his wife as she held Hans in her arms. "But I must go, and you must be brave," he added quietly. "Pray for me the whole time I'm gone. The man is coming to meet me this afternoon, and from there we'll be—"

But Betteken felt she had heard enough. Overcome with fear, she jumped up. Father stopped short, a surprised look crossing his face. Betteken ran to the stairway, her breath coming in gasps as she cried, "I don't want you to go!"

Without waiting for an answer, she ran up the stairs. She felt she had to be alone right now. She wished she were under her bed covers, just waking up from a nightmare. If only it were possible! If Father went to Ghent, what horrible things would happen to him?

---

[1] Ministers in the sixteenth century often traveled to teach and preach in other cities and villages.

Throwing herself across the bed, she buried her face in her pillow.

. . . .

"Betteken?"

The voice was soft and comfortingly close. Slowly, Betteken raised her head from the pillow. Her eyes were red from crying, and strands of blond hair hung loose about her face. Sitting down on the bed beside her, Mama gently stroked her hair.

"I know how you feel, Betty." She paused, and Betteken scooted closer. Mama put one arm around her. "I'm afraid for Father too. His work is dangerous. But remember that he's doing what God has called him to do. And God will take care of him."

"How do you know, Mama?" Betteken whispered against her shoulder. "How do you know that God will keep Father safe?"

"Father will not come to harm unless God lets it happen, and then we will know that He has a reason for doing so." Tipping up Betteken's chin, Mama looked into her eyes. "It's not our job to worry about the future; it's our job to learn to love and trust our heavenly Father."

Pulling back, Betteken looked into her mother's face. "How can you be so sure?"

A smile touched Maeyken's lips. "God is much bigger than you can imagine, dear. He wouldn't ask this of Father if He didn't know that something beautiful will come out of it. And God is more than able to keep Father safe. Even if he goes to prison."

Betteken was silent for a moment. "Mama," she said at last. "I saw a face in the window last night when Adriaen and I were talking in the parlor. Do you think it was the man from Ghent?"

"It's possible," Maeyken said slowly. "He came soon after you and Adriaen went to bed. But I can't say for sure that it was him."

"Do you think our house is being watched?"

"I hope not. But try not to worry, Betty. Remember, God is with us."

They sat in silence for a while longer. Betteken wished she could stay in Mama's arms forever. She felt safe, as though nothing could hurt her as long as she was there.

"Betteken." Mama was speaking again, her voice soft and low. "God wants to hold you, just like I'm holding you right now. God will hold all of us like that if we only let Him. He holds us close to His heart and gives us peace, no matter what."

Betteken did not answer. But she felt the peace in Mama's words and knew she was right. Father was needed in Ghent. They would pray for him, and he would be in God's care.

CHAPTER FIVE

Johannes the Printer

Adriaen always enjoyed working with his father, who often sang or whistled cheerfully. Sometimes they discussed the best way to lay freestone for building, or heavier issues like the war between Spain and the Lowlands. But today Father was silent.

Adriaen didn't feel like talking either. He worked beside his father, laying the freestone with the ease of long practice. But his thoughts were far away.

His father had been a minister for as long as Adriaen could remember. He often traveled from place to place, baptizing, preaching, and teaching people about the Lord. Adriaen sometimes wished he could be home more often. The uncertainty of his lifestyle was wearing. They never knew when their father would be called away.

It was nearing noon when Mattheus finally packed up his tools. "Let's go home for the noon meal," he said.

Adriaen's heartbeat quickened. He knew his father would leave shortly after the meal. How long would it be before

BETTEKEN'S REFUGE

he came home again?

The meal seemed too short. Mattheus picked up his traveling bundle and bid his family goodbye. Then he turned and spoke to Adriaen. "Follow me, son."

They walked out the back door to the small barn behind the courtyard, and Adriaen helped his father saddle the horse. Most of the peasants were too poor to own a horse, but Father needed one for his travels.

As Mattheus led his horse outside, he spoke with Adriaen one last time. "You're the man of the family while I'm gone, Adriaen," he said softly. "Take care of your mother and sister and little brother. Be strong for them."

Adriaen looked up. "I will, Father."

"I know." Mattheus smiled and clasped his shoulder. "Goodbye, son. I'm depending on you."

"Goodbye." Adriaen stood still, watching as his father mounted the horse. He flicked the reins, and they disappeared into the crowd.

When Adriaen turned, Mama was standing behind him in the open doorway. "Aren't you coming in?"

"I'm coming." But he lingered a moment longer. There was no sound from the house, and he found himself wishing that he could be a little boy again, safe in his mother's arms until all of this was over.

But Father had said that he was the man of the family now. Squaring his shoulders, Adriaen followed his mother inside.

Betteken stood at the fireplace, keeping watch over the boiling soap in the iron pot. Aunt Margretha was coming this morning to help clean the house. Betteken looked forward to her arrival. Her aunt always seemed to have a merry heart.

She checked the pot once more and turned. "I think it's ready now, Mama."

Maeyken set down the buckets of water she had brought from the well, brushing a wisp of dark hair from her face. Betteken often thought her mother looked young. There were no gray threads in her hair like there were in Father's. But now her eyes looked tired. "Set the pot aside to cool, then. I'll pour it into the molds after a little bit. You've done a good job of making that soap, Betteken."

The smile she gave Betteken made the kitchen seem brighter. Betteken hummed softly as she swung the iron rod out from over the fireplace and lifted the pot. She stirred it one last time and set it beside the hearth.

The door opened, and a cold gust of wind swept into the kitchen. "It smells like soap in here! I think I've come to the right place." Aunt Margretha came inside, her cheeks flushed a rosy color from her walk in the winter air. Her dark eyes sparkled. "Put me to work, Maeyken!"

That was Aunt Margretha—always keeping the house alive with her cheer. Betteken wished her aunt could live with them all the time. If she knew how worried they all felt about Father, she didn't show it.

It was a week now since their father had left—the longest week Betteken could ever remember. Though they tried to act normal, there was always a sense of *waiting*. Waiting until Father came home again and they knew he was safe. Waiting until he would complete their family circle once more.

Betteken glanced longingly out the window. They watched the streets every day, but always it was only Adriaen that she saw, leaving in the morning or coming home at night. Working without Father's help left him so exhausted that he often went to bed right after supper. He seemed to be growing older right before her eyes.

"Betteken!"

Aunt Margretha's voice jerked her back to reality. Her aunt was standing beside her, holding her hand level with Betteken's head. "You're nearly as tall as I am! When did you start becoming such a lady?"

Mama smiled. "I've been lengthening her skirts again. It seems as though she outgrows her frocks as soon as I make them!"

Betteken blushed slightly but laughed with the others. "You really aren't that tall, Aunt Margretha," she said. "I might even become taller than you!"

"Aunt 'Etha!" Hans raced into the kitchen and flung his arms around her. "Stay for supper, stay for supper!"

She laughed and swept him up into her arms. "What would your mama say?"

"That's fine with me," Maeyken answered without hesitation. "We'd love to have you stay." She picked up a bucket and a bar of soap. "Get two rags, Betteken, and Aunt Margretha will help you dust upstairs. I'll be working down here."

Hans followed them up the stairs, staying at Aunt Margretha's side as she dusted Adriaen's room. Betteken then went to her own room across the hall and wiped down all the dusty surfaces. As she worked, she could hear Aunt Margretha singing. Though he didn't know the words, Hans tried to sing along. His sweet treble made Betteken smile. Throwing open the shutters at the window, she leaned out, looking down the narrow street.

From where she stood, the city seemed to be asleep. Only a few people here and there hurried along the cobbled streets, and she could see a team of horses pulling a wagon. But then she heard a sound that made her tremble.

Swinging around, she hurried to Adriaen's room. His window overlooked another part of the street, where the sound was coming from. Aunt Margretha was already watching, holding Hans in her arms. She glanced back as Betteken came into the room, and her face was more sober than Betteken had ever seen it.

"What's happening?" Betteken exclaimed.

Her aunt didn't answer but made room for her at the window. Betteken leaned forward, peering through the window. Spanish soldiers were marching through the street to the city gates. In their midst stumbled a young man in chains. A crowd was gathering, closing them in on all sides. Betteken's face blanched as she saw the man's face.

"It's Johannes the printer!" she whispered.

Johannes worked at a printing press, where they published many books and flyers. Betteken knew that he also printed

Anabaptist tracts and booklets for the Christians. Father often carried a few tracts, hidden in a pocket of his overcoat. If an Anabaptist carrying such material was arrested, he would be in serious trouble.

But it also meant serious trouble if the printer of that literature was caught. Printing Anabaptist literature was against the law. "Was he caught printing something illegal?" she asked Aunt Margretha.

Her aunt knew what she meant. "It's possible. Look at Johannes—his lips are moving. I wonder what he's saying."

But Betteken's gaze riveted on a figure darting through the crowd. The young man had Adriaen's blond hair, and he was working his way close to the soldiers and their prisoner. Wanting to know if it was indeed Adriaen, she leaned closer, but the procession was already turning the corner. In another moment they would be out of sight.

Without a second thought, she turned and left the room. Mama was nowhere in sight when she dashed through the kitchen. Closing the door behind her, Betteken hurried down the street.

The soldiers and their prisoner were nearing the city gates. In the press of the crowd, Betteken could hardly see the two guards setting up a stake with wood around it. Breaking into a run, she circled behind and dodged through openings between the people until she was close to the front.

The young printer was now being led to the stake. His dark eyes held a mixture of apprehension and peace, but Betteken could hear him singing softly as the guards fastened him to the wood.

A man stepped forward, a flaming torch in his hand. Johannes saw him and grew still. Then Betteken saw him lift his face toward the clouds above him. His lips moved again, and to Betteken it seemed he was surrendering himself to God in that moment.

As the executioner lowered the torch to set the wood on

fire, Betteken saw the blond head again. It was certainly her brother. He was standing on the other side of the stocks, talking to one of the soldiers. Turning, she darted through the crowd until she was close enough to hear.

"What has he done?" she heard Adriaen asking. "What crime has he committed?"

"He printed something illegal." The soldier spat on the ground, almost hitting Betteken's feet. She jumped back and glanced at her brother. He didn't seem to notice her. "He printed that literature that the heretics are forever reading," the soldier went on. "He deserved this!"

Betteken looked at his hard eyes and felt chilled. She didn't want to stay here any longer. Adriaen started toward her, but she didn't wait for him. She only knew that she had to get away from this place.

Adriaen caught up with her when she turned into their empty home street. "Betteken, I wish you wouldn't have seen that."

"Neither do I."

"He didn't do anything wrong, you know."

"I know." She hesitated, hardly able to speak around the hard knot in her throat. "They do such horrible things, Adriaen."

"The Spaniards think that anyone who isn't part of the state church is a threat to the system, even those who are just sympathetic," he reminded her. A troubled look came over his face. "I saw them bring Johannes out of prison."

She glanced up with a start. "You did?"

"I was working at the street corner when they came through

49

the gates. They were all shouting that he was a heretic, but he was silent."

With a tremor in her voice, Betteken said, "You were brave to speak to that soldier."

"Perhaps I was more foolhardy than brave. If he would think I was sympathetic . . ." His voice trailed off.

Behind them, the hubbub of the crowd grew fainter. Betteken was glad to enter the house and shut the door, blocking it out altogether.

CHAPTER SIX

The Stranger's Message

That afternoon Betteken set out to visit Elizabeth. The streets were calmer now, though the people still seemed restless from what had happened earlier. Betteken felt relieved when the weaver's shop came into view.

Only Elizabeth was in the room when she entered. Her face lit up when she saw Betteken. "I was hoping you'd come."

"How are you feeling, Elizabeth?" Betteken asked, coming to her side.

"Better. Mama is taking good care of me." She leaned forward. "Betteken, I saw everything from my window."

"You mean the printer's execution?"

Elizabeth nodded, her eyes flashing with anger. "I could hardly bear to watch. How can they be so cruel?"

"The authorities would say they were doing their duty," Betteken said hesitantly.

"But it's not right!" Elizabeth took a deep breath. "Perhaps Johannes did print something illegal, but he didn't deserve to be put to death. I really admire people who stand up for what they believe, especially the Anabaptists." Glancing up, she searched Betteken's face. "What do you think of all this? I know it's the law to get rid of them, but it's a horrid law! I wish there were some way to change it."

Betteken nodded and murmured agreement, although she didn't want to say too much.

Elizabeth's voice softened. "My mother wants to learn more about the Anabaptists. She really admires them."

Betteken caught her breath. "She does?"

"She isn't satisfied with the Catholic church." Elizabeth stopped, and a worried look came into her eyes. "I shouldn't be telling you this. Betteken, please don't tell anyone."

"I won't," Betteken promised. "But how would your mother find out what she wants to know?"

Elizabeth shrugged slightly. "I'm not sure who she would talk to, but I want her to be careful. I told her so, and she said that she isn't doing anything rash. She'll take her time."

Minutes later, Betteken said goodbye to Elizabeth and hurried home, avoiding the plaza where the execution had taken place.

. . . .

Soft light from the oil lamp spilled over the room. Maeyken sat at her spinning wheel close to the fire, fastening fibers of wool on a distaff to spin into thread. She had said she would teach Betteken how to spin sometime that winter, but for now Betteken was content to watch.

THE STRANGER'S MESSAGE

Aunt Margretha came into the room, fastening her cloak. "It's time for me to leave, Maeyken," she said. "I wanted to be home before dark, and it is twilight now."

Mama didn't answer immediately. For a moment the only sound in the room was the hum of her spinning wheel. Then she spoke quietly without looking up. "I wonder where Mattheus is right now. All day I've been praying for him."

Betteken swallowed hard. In her mind's eye she could still see the soldiers dragging the printer through the street, and the executioner stepping forward with a flaming torch. Surely nothing like that would happen to Father . . . would it?

Aunt Margretha turned slowly. "Has he ever been gone this long before?"

Mama shook her head. "Usually he's home within a couple days. But it's been a week now, and he still isn't back."

The family fell silent, concern showing in their eyes. At length Aunt Margretha suggested, "Why don't we pray together for him right now?"

Mama smiled faintly. "That's a good idea. Will you pray for us?"

In answer, Aunt Margretha bowed her head. "Heavenly Father, we come to you in Jesus' name." Her voice was hushed and reverent, and Betteken felt better just listening to her. "We pray now that you will keep Mattheus safe. If he's in danger, please protect him and bring him home to his family again. Most of all, we pray that your will be done."

When she finished praying, Mama's face looked peaceful. "God is in control," she said softly. "We can rest."

Aunt Margretha stepped to the door. "I must go now. Take care."

"Be careful out on those streets, Margretha," Maeyken said. "People are still restless from what happened today."

Adriaen jumped up. "I'll walk you home."

"I'd appreciate that." Aunt Margretha looked relieved. "I really wasn't looking forward to walking home all by myself."

As the door closed behind them, Betteken watched her mother sit down at her spinning wheel again. "I wish I could be brave like you, Mama," she said suddenly.

Her mother looked up. "What do you mean, Betty?"

"Well . . ." Betteken hesitated. "You don't ever get afraid."

Mama smiled a little. "Oh, Betteken, I do get afraid. But praying gives me the courage I need to go on." The spinning wheel slowed. "It strengthens my faith in God."

"I wish I could have faith like that." Betteken absently smoothed her skirt.

"You can, dear. If you confess your sins and decide to follow Jesus, He will give you faith to believe in His power. And you'll have peace about Father."

"Even if he *dies?*" The word was so blunt and harsh that Betteken caught her breath.

"Father will be *more* than all right if that happens, Betteken. He's a Christian, and he'll go to heaven. There's no pain, suffering, or sorrow there." Mama's voice choked a little. "We'd miss him here, of course, but we would know that he's in a better place."

Betteken was quiet, deep in thought. She had heard much about heaven—how beautiful it was and how happy everyone would be there. Father and Mama both spoke of it often.

Mama's voice broke into her reverie. "How was your visit with Elizabeth today?"

Betteken met her gaze. "She said that she really admires the believers, and the law to get rid of them is a horrid law." She fell silent, wishing she could say what Elizabeth had told her about her mother. But she had promised not to.

Mama looked thoughtful. "This world is a sinful place," she said softly. "But the Bible says we need to trust God. Trusting gives us courage."

Betteken glanced out the window. Somewhere in that inky darkness was her father. Was he even now running through the woods, fleeing from captors? She shook her head to keep herself from thinking such thoughts. Her mind turned to Adriaen and Aunt Margretha, walking through the streets. At least they were safe . . . she hoped. After what had happened to the printer, it seemed as though danger lurked at every corner.

. . . .

Adriaen was glad for the chance to be alone after he left Aunt Margretha and started walking home. Watching his mother and aunt pray had left him feeling confused. *He* should have been the one to pray, to be strong for his mother. "The man of the family," Father had said. How could he be a man, though, when he didn't have the faith that Mama had?

He'd turned into his street when he heard the sound of a horse's hoof beats behind him. The darkness made the rider in the saddle a dim silhouette. His hat was pulled low over his face.

The farther Adriaen went, the closer those hoof beats came. He stopped and listened hard. He was almost home now. Was that the place this rider was seeking?

He didn't think it was Father riding the horse. He hesitated before turning around furtively to look. The rider was passing him now, and he didn't look like Father.

THE STRANGER'S MESSAGE

Adriaen decided to run, but he would do so behind the houses instead of in the street. He stepped into an alley and broke into a sprint. When he opened the back door of their house moments later, the horse was approaching their gate.

Stepping inside, he spoke quickly to Mama. "There's someone here. I don't know who it is, but I'm going to see." Taking the lantern, he went out the front door. "Who's there?" he called.

"Is this the house of Mattheus Wens?" The rider stopped his horse in the circle of light made by the lantern.

"Yes, sir." Uneasiness coiled within him. How did this stranger know his father? But then, Father knew many people from his travels.

"I have something to tell you about your father," the stranger said. "But I don't want to talk about it out here."

"Of course. Come inside." Adriaen led the way into the kitchen. Maeyken stood up from her spinning wheel, her face pale. "What is this about, sir?"

The stranger held up his hand. "As far as I know, your husband is all right. But it may be a few days before he gets home." He hesitated, his glance taking in Betteken, who was sitting by the fire with Hans in her arms. His voice softened. "We were discovered at our meeting a few nights ago. Some were captured, but others escaped. Your husband was among those who escaped."

Maeyken's tense expression eased a little. "Where is he now?" she asked quietly.

"He's been hiding at our house. But he wanted to let you know what happened, so I came to tell you." He looked at Maeyken soberly. "Since the soldiers are still looking for him, it isn't safe for him to come home yet."

There was a long silence as the family members took in the news. Finally Maeyken nodded. "Thank you so much for coming," she said gratefully. "Will you allow me to heat a drink for you before you start out again?"

"No, I must hurry on." The man backed toward the door. "I

stopped in only long enough to tell you about your husband."

"Please accept a fresh loaf of bread as a token of my appreciation," Maeyken said. "You will need it to nourish you on your ride home."

When the stranger was gone, Adriaen stepped close to his mother. "Do you know who he was?"

A smile lit Maeyken's face. "He's the stranger who came for Father that night after you and Betteken were both in bed. I was worried about what news he was bringing. But God answered our prayers! Let's thank Him right now."

Adriaen's confusion returned as he knelt with the others. Mama believed in God so simply and completely. Would he ever be able to claim her faith as his own?

CHAPTER SEVEN

Father's Return

The day Father came home always stood out vividly in Betteken's memory.

The skies were a crystal blue that day, and the sun attempted to warm the grass where she was helping her mother wash laundry. Hans romped around them, his blond curls ruffling in the March wind.

Adriaen whistled a clear tune as he sat on the steps nearby, whittling a wooden horse for his little brother. He had completed the masonry contract they'd been working on when his father left, so he had time now to spend with the family. Except for her worry about Father, it was a day that made Betteken feel good all over.

Mama was spreading underclothes across the grass to dry when they heard a horse's hooves coming down the street. "Adriaen, could you check to see if you know who that is?" she asked.

Betteken also wanted to know, so she stood up and followed her brother to the front of the house. A horse and rider were coming toward them. When the rider raised a hand in greeting, she knew. "Father!" she shouted, breaking into a run. As she opened the gate, her father quickly dismounted his horse. "Oh, Father, you're back!" was all Betteken could choke out.

Mattheus laughed and swung his daughter around in a circle, as though she were as light as Hans. "I could hardly wait to get home and see all of you again!"

And then Mama was there, with Hans hurrying after her. Everyone laughed and talked at once, until Mama remembered the laundry still waiting at the back of the house. "We'll finish what's in the tub, and then we're done for today," she declared, her eyes sparkling. "This afternoon Betteken and I are going to make a special cake for supper!"

Betteken hadn't known how weighty her fear was until it was gone. "I'll finish the laundry for you, Mama," she offered. She felt as though she were floating a few inches above the ground as she ran back to the house. Father and Adriaen headed to the barn with the horse. When she was finished, Betteken hurried to join them.

"This little mare has had a long, hard trip," Father was saying when she came into the barn. "But she did a good job."

Adriaen smiled as he rubbed one hand over the horse's coat. "I'm so glad you're safely home, Father."

"And how about you, Betteken?" Father winked at her.

She laughed. "Everything is just right when you're here with us."

Betteken watched them a moment longer before moving

toward the house. Mama was already working on the cake. First she mixed together roasted pears, shelled almonds, curds, and mashed raisins. After spicing the mixture with sugar and cinnamon, she allowed Betteken to beat the eggs and add fresh butter. Finally the cake baked over the fire, its sweet smell filling the house and making Betteken's mouth water.

When the cake was done, Mama set it aside to cool and quickly prepared a stew for the main course of the meal. As she hung the kettle to simmer over the fire, Mama smiled at Betteken. "I'll help you set the table tonight, Betty. Bring the rose-colored tablecloth."

Betteken's eyes widened. Mama never used that tablecloth except for special company and holidays. Mama saw her surprise and laughed. "This is a special night, Betteken. Father is safely at home! That's reason to celebrate, don't you think?"

Betteken ran to the parlor, where Mama kept the neatly folded tablecloth in a cupboard. Its rich rose color made the kitchen seem like a palace when it was spread out on the table. Mama lit two candles and placed them in the center. The flickering flames cast cozy shadows over the whole room.

Hans danced around the kitchen, clapping his hands. "It's bootiful, Mama!"

"So it is, little son," she answered, laughing. "We'll be dining like kings tonight." Then she turned back to the hearth to check her stew.

Supper that night was more relaxing than any they'd had in their father's absence. Betteken sat beside Adriaen on the bench and thought she must be the happiest girl in the world.

After the dishes were washed and put away, the family gathered near the fire. Mama sat down at her spinning wheel while Father gathered his children close. "It's so good to be home again," he said, smiling. "I've missed these long evenings with my family."

Mama glanced up, a smile glowing deep in her eyes.

"The stranger told us that some of you were captured at the meeting," Adriaen spoke up.

Father nodded, but he didn't seem to want to talk about it. "The Lord protected us," he said simply. "But at our meeting was a man who served under the High Bailiff of Ghent."

Mama gasped. "Did he betray you?"

Father shook his head, and his smile deepened. "The man's name was Anthonis Ysbaerts. He often attended the executions of the Christians at Ghent. Eventually it affected him so much that he decided to leave his position under the bailiff and follow Christ. He asked for baptism the night I was there."

His voice filled with wonder, Father continued. "Think of it. He knows all about what the believers face, yet he was willing to accept our faith as his own. I talked with him just before I left this morning. He is planning to flee to Friesland—it's too dangerous for him to remain where he is now. It's unlikely he'll be able to earn much of a living there, but his strength is amazing. He's willing to leave everything he's ever known for Christ's sake."

"That is beautiful," Mama said softly.

"I would like to tell Anthonis's story at our next meeting," Father said. "I think it would encourage the church here to keep the faith."[1]

As the fire died down to glowing embers, Father took out his Bible and flipped carefully through its pages. "There's a certain verse I'd like to share with you that comforted me while I was gone," he said, glancing up. "It's the first verse in Psalm 27: 'The LORD is my light and my salvation; whom shall I fear? The LORD is the strength of my life; of whom shall I be afraid?' "

He paused. "The Lord is on our side, and there is nothing to fear. No person or situation can shake our strength when we trust Him. In God we find refuge for our souls."

Betteken glanced at Adriaen. He was staring into the fire, his blue eyes unreadable. She wondered what he was thinking. As for herself, she was thrilled by the power of Father's story and the words he was sharing from the Bible. Yes, their way of life was hard. But they had God on their side, and that was enough.

. . . .

Alone in her room, Betteken set her candle on the block stool next to her bed and unbraided her hair. In the dim light it shone like gold. As she brushed it out, she tried to imagine what Anthonis Ysbaerts had gone through. She knew it had taken great courage for him to give up his former way of life for the sake of Christ.

---
[1] The story of Anthonis Ysbaerts is found on pages 991–992 in the *Martyrs Mirror*.

Setting down her brush, she stepped over to her open door, ready to close it for the night. The low murmur of voices below reached her. "What happened, Mattheus?" Mama was asking.

Betteken stopped short. From the top of the stairs, she could see her parents sitting together before the fire. Neither of them had seen her. She was about to close her door when Father's words caught her attention.

"The meeting was held in a lofted barn," he said in a hushed tone. "I baptized four people: two women, Anthonis Ysbaerts, and a boy Adriaen's age. We were praying when we heard horses' hooves galloping toward us outside."

Betteken heard Mama catch her breath as her father went on. "As the soldiers emerged from the trees, our host opened the lower window and let the women and children get out first. Others escaped through the loft window, sliding down tree branches just outside. I was the last to follow the women and children before the soldiers crashed through the door. They captured a group of about ten people."

Father gazed into the flames. "Two of the prisoners recanted," he said quietly. "One of them was the young boy I had just baptized."

"Oh, Mattheus," Mama breathed.

Father's eyes glistened with unshed tears. "He was only Adriaen's age, Maeyken. He feared death. I pray that God will have mercy on his soul."

Betteken didn't stay to hear more. She closed the door without a sound and climbed into bed, shaking from more than the cold as she pulled the bed covers up to her chin. She had always known that Father was in danger when he traveled to other places, but she'd never heard him tell a story like this before.

She lay in bed a long time, staring into the darkness until sleep claimed her.

CHAPTER EIGHT

Whom Shall I Fear?

*A*driaen couldn't sleep.

He tossed and turned in his bed, his mind replaying many scenes. The execution of Johannes the printer. Father's dangerous trip. Other deaths of believers that had taken place in the city. Many of them he didn't know, but they had been bonded together by one common goal: to live or die for Christ.

Why did God allow these things to happen? Where was His love—His mercy—in their suffering and constant danger?

He thought of Betteken. His younger sister's face was so open and honest, her blue eyes either shadowed with quiet worry or sparkling with the joy of life. She was much like Mama. Was he like Father? He wanted to be. But was it possible if he didn't have his father's faith?

Slipping out of bed, he knelt on the floor and buried his face in his hands. The minutes grew long, and soon he was shivering with cold. Still he waited.

But no answers came to his questions. No sense of peace

descended on his spirit. There was only silence.

. . . .

Betteken held Hans's small hand as they walked down the street. The day was clear and sunny, and a late snow laced the tall stone houses. "Next month is April, and we'll see signs of spring," she told Hans. "I can hardly wait."

Hans glanced up, a question in his eyes. "Spring?"

"When it turns warm and the flowers bloom," she explained. "When we won't have to wear cloaks anymore and can run barefoot through the grass." Just thinking about it made her heart leap.

Hans pointed to a bird dipping and soaring overhead. "Will we fly?"

"Oh, Hans!" Betteken's laughter made several ladies passing by glance over and smile. "What made you think of that? But yes, I think our spirits will fly."

"Our spirits?" Hans was lost again.

"How we feel inside. Our hearts will sing!" They were entering the main part of the city now. Teams of horses passed by in a blur, and Betteken pulled Hans to one side. "We need to stay over here to walk."

Hans skipped along beside her, chattering happily about many things. Betteken shifted the basket in her hand, her face sobering. She thought again of her father's near-capture. She hadn't talked about it with her parents. Somehow it seemed that if she avoided the subject of her father's dangerous lifestyle, nothing bad would happen to him.

WHOM SHALL I FEAR?

"Hi there!"

Betteken glanced up sharply. Aunt Margretha was sweeping snow off the steps of the house where she lived with her parents. "You looked deep in thought," she said with a smile.

Betteken managed to smile back. "I went to pick up an order of wool for Mama."

"Come in for a little while," Aunt Margretha suggested, opening the door.

Grandma's kitchen smelled like freshly baked bread. Her apron was finely dusted with flour, and her smile was warm. "It's been awhile since I've seen you two," she said, hugging Betteken and Hans. "Here, sit down and eat some fresh bread. What's been happening in your life these days?"

Hans answered first. "Father came home yes'erday! And we had cake for supper!"

"You did?" She smiled down at him. "It's special to have him home, isn't it?"

"I wish he'd never have to leave again," Betteken said.

Grandma looked at her kindly. "You love him very much, don't you?"

Betteken didn't answer, and a thoughtful look came into Grandma's eyes. Setting down her bread knife, she held out her hand. "I want to show you something, Betteken."

She led the way upstairs to her bedroom. There she took her Bible from under the mattress of her bed and opened it carefully. "I want to share a verse with you that has helped calm me through these times. It's the first verse in Psalm 27: 'The LORD is my light and my salvation; whom shall

I fear? The LORD is the strength of my life; of whom shall I be afraid?'"

Betteken stood very still. Did this verse hold a special meaning? Father had shared it in their family devotions the night before, and now Grandma was talking about it.

Grandma placed a hand on Betteken's shoulder. "Just treasure your times together. And why don't you memorize this verse for yourself?"

Betteken couldn't speak. But Grandma, her eyes soft with love, seemed to understand.

. . . .

The meeting place on Joos Marten's farm was hidden deep in the forest outside the city gates. Shadowy figures slipped through the darkness to gather there in the dim light of a lantern.

Adriaen stood with Pieter near the creek rippling quietly by. Knowing that his friend had requested baptism this night, Adriaen glanced sideways at him now and then. Once Pieter met his eyes and smiled. He seemed to feel peaceful. But Adriaen couldn't shake off his uneasiness.

He admired Pieter for his quiet confidence that he was doing the right thing. His friend had vowed to follow Jesus, no matter the cost. But now Adriaen felt tense. After his father's close call, it seemed that persecution was closer than it had ever been before.

Father moved close to the light and held up his Bible. His voice was strong. "In Galatians chapter three, there's a verse that says, 'For as many of you as have been baptized into Christ have put on Christ.' The young man before us has repented of his sins and now desires to be baptized. By this outward sign of the covenant, he will testify publicly that he has put off the old man and put on the new."

Father glanced around the circle. "When you repent from your sins, you become spiritually reborn, and wake from death to life. God will transform you into a new creature, from a sinful man into one at peace in Christ. Through faith in the Gospel of Jesus and the power of the Holy Spirit, your life can be renewed, and you, too, can be ready for baptism."

He paused, and Adriaen felt his pulse quicken. To accept this gift of salvation would mean freedom. He would be free from his guilt, free to simply trust in God. Why was he holding back?

Without warning, the thunder of horses' hooves came on the wind. In seconds, soldiers were charging into the clearing, yelling and waving clubs.

There was no time to think. Adriaen snatched up Hans and ran toward the trees. Betteken followed, glancing back just before they plunged into the deep darkness. All but five of the believers had escaped. As she caught sight of a familiar figure in the small group, Betteken froze.

"Betteken!" Adriaen whispered. "We have to run!" Reaching back, he took her hand and led the way homeward. She stumbled along behind him, her quiet sobs tearing at his heart.

Father was waiting for them when they arrived home. He said nothing—just drew all three of them close and held them tight. Adriaen knew then that he too had seen Mama among the prisoners.

. . . .

After the others were in bed, Betteken slipped out of her room and went downstairs. Father kept his Bible hidden in the cupboard, but he'd said that they could use it whenever they wished. She carried it carefully to the kitchen, where the fire was burning low in the hearth. It gave just enough light to see the words in Father's Bible.

She opened to the book of Psalms, searching until she found the verse that Father and Grandma had spoken of. She traced one finger over the words that talked of having nothing to fear when the Lord is the strength of your life.

The ache in her heart was nearly unbearable. "Dear God," she whispered. "Will you please let Mama come home again?" Fresh tears welled up in her eyes, falling unheeded down her cheeks. "Father just came home a week ago, and now Mama's in prison. I don't want her to die!"

On the page in front of her eyes, four words blurred and cleared. *Whom shall I fear?*

"God will hold all of us if we only let Him," Mama had said once. "He holds us close to His heart and gives us peace, no matter what."

"The Lord is on our side, and we have nothing to fear," Father had said. "No person or situation can shake our strength when we are trusting Him. In God we find refuge for our souls."

Whom shall I fear? Betteken stared down at the words and felt hope steal into her heart. When at last she closed the Bible, the flow of her tears had stopped and a faint smile lit her face.

CHAPTER NINE

Adriaen's Questions

The kitchen that morning was cold and silent. Normally Mama would be up, fanning the fire and cooking breakfast. Betteken stood for a moment in the doorway, wishing she could run back upstairs again. Facing this day without Mama was going to be hard.

What made things even worse was that their father was in grave danger, especially if he stayed here. Now that Mama had been captured, it could be only a matter of time before the authorities found her husband too.

In that instant, she felt a hand on her shoulder. Father was looking down at her with something very sorrowful in his smile. "Adriaen and I will help you all we can, Betty."

Standing next to his father, Adriaen nodded. "We still have each other, and we'll have to work together."

Mattheus looked pleased. "That's the spirit." He stepped over to the hearth to light the fire. "I'll slice a loaf of bread for breakfast," he said as flames danced up. "We don't need much. But later this morning, I'll ask Aunt Margretha to come over and help us out."

Betteken's throat choked up so that she could hardly speak. "Will Mama ever come home again, Father?"

There was pain in his eyes when he looked at her. "I don't know, Betty. Shall we pray together about it?"

They had already prayed together the night before, and Betteken had awakened numerous times during the night and prayed until she fell asleep again. "It would make me feel better," she said now.

Mattheus smiled. "I'm glad you find strength in prayer. We should pray without ceasing."

A small whimper caught their attention. Hans stood in the doorway of his father's room, clutching his blanket, his blue eyes wide and frightened. "Where's Mama?" he asked.

Mattheus quickly stepped over to his youngest son and swept him up in his arms. "She isn't here, Hans." He swallowed hard and ran one hand through Hans's blond curls. "We'll pray that she can come home again, all right?"

Hans nodded and leaned his head against his father's shoulder. Mattheus closed his eyes and spoke in a hushed voice. "Dear Lord, you know what has happened to Mama and how much we miss her. Will you keep her safe and bring her home again to us? Nevertheless, not our will, but thine be done."

Betteken wondered how God would answer Father's prayer. She thought of it often as the day wore on. This was even worse than when Father traveled to preach in distant cities. What was Mama doing in that prison? Would she ever be released and allowed to come home again?

ADRIAEN'S QUESTIONS

The sun was high in the sky when Aunt Margretha came. She swept Hans into her arms and drew Betteken close, holding her tight. Betteken buried her face in her aunt's apron and cried. They stayed that way for a long time.

. . . .

The five prisoners had been placed in two cells, Hans Munstdorp in one and the four women in the other. Maeyken Wens knelt on the cold stone floor, her hands covering her face. "My dear husband and children need me, Lord," she pleaded silently. "They need me . . ." Her prayer broke into sobs that shook her frame.

A gentle arm slipped around her shoulder, and Janneken Munstdorp spoke softly. "Take courage, friend. You are not alone."

The other two women, Mariken and Lijsken, knelt beside them. They prayed together, lifting their hearts to God. He heard, and tenderly He showered His gifts of love and peace upon them.

. . . .

Adriaen threw himself fiercely into his work, a dark cloud on his brow. What had Betteken said? *Praying makes me feel better.* He didn't even feel like trying to pray. If God truly cared about them . . .

He jerked open the chest of tools. If God was so kind and loving, why did He allow people like his mother to get captured? She hadn't done anything to deserve it. And they needed her. Father, Betteken, little Hans—they all needed her. It wasn't fair!

His father had stayed home today, saying he needed to fast and pray. Their present situation looked dark, and the future looked even darker. It made Adriaen feel sick at heart.

At the supper table that night, Adriaen only picked at his smoked herring, and he knew the others did too. When Father brought his Bible to the table, he straightened. Perhaps Father would read something that could help him feel better.

Mattheus read that night from the book of Matthew. "Blessed are ye, when men shall revile you, and persecute you, and shall say all manner of evil against you falsely, for my sake. Rejoice, and be exceeding glad: for great is your reward in heaven: for so persecuted they the prophets which were before you."

He paused and glanced at Adriaen. "I think these are good verses for you to remember, son. And for all of us," he added, glancing around the table. "Mama is in prison, but we know that it's because she loves God. When we suffer for His sake, we can rejoice because our reward will be great."

"Father?" Hans's voice was small. "I want Mama to come home again."

"We all do, son," Father answered tenderly. "And we'll pray that God will allow it to happen. But we also need to remember that God is with her, and He will do what is best."

Adriaen stared unseeingly into the fire. How could God be doing what was best when his mother was in prison?

"Adriaen?" Betteken was standing in the open doorway when he turned. "What are you doing?"

Adriaen didn't answer. Looking puzzled, she came to stand beside him at the window. "What are you looking at? I don't see anything unusual down there on the street."

"I'm not looking at the street."

"Oh." Understanding dawned in her blue eyes. "You're looking at the prison." She studied it silently for a moment. "What do you think Mama is doing tonight?"

Adriaen shrugged. "Trying to sleep, perhaps." He closed the shutters with a bang. "Or praying. I'm not sure that praying will do any good, though."

"Adriaen!"

"We might as well face up to it, Betteken." His voice was just above a whisper now. "Mama is in prison, and we don't know that we'll ever see her again."

She caught her breath. "But we must have faith that God will—"

"That God will what?" he challenged, turning his face away from her. "The authorities are determined to do away with us. They think we're committing treason. Where is God in it all?"

She was silent for a long moment. "Father is always saying that God is a refuge for our souls. Don't you believe it?"

He ran his fingers restlessly through his hair. "I want to. But nothing makes sense to me anymore."

Adriaen lay awake that night again, staring into the darkness.

CHAPTER TEN

Why Pray?

Betteken and Aunt Margretha walked down the street, heading toward the marketplace. Betteken felt ill at ease, as though they might be looked upon with suspicion at any moment. But the only person who seemed to notice them was a richly tailored woman, who lifted her skirts—and her nose—as she swept by.

"Are you going to visit Elizabeth today?" Aunt Margretha asked.

Betteken shook her head firmly. "Not today."

"Why not?"

"Father Wils . . ." Betteken stopped and swallowed hard. "He was there once when I visited Elizabeth." The last thing she wanted was for the priest to discover who she was.

Aunt Margretha was quiet for a moment. "He likely won't be there, but if he is . . ." She paused. "Elizabeth would soon notice if you never came to visit. I'll go with you, if you like."

They were entering a shop now, and Betteken could only whisper, "Thanks. I'd like that."

Minutes later, they approached the Wils house. Elizabeth's mother met them at the door, and her eyes lit up. "I'm so glad you're here," she said. "Please come in."

Elizabeth was sitting near the hearth, her face pale. She took hold of Betteken's hand. "I'm so sorry about what happened to your mother, Betteken," she said softly.

Betteken felt the familiar tears sting her eyes. "How did you know, Elizabeth?"

"My uncle told us the names of those in prison." Elizabeth squeezed her hand. "I'm so sorry."

"I want you to know that I'm willing to help you in any way I can," Elizabeth's mother said, coming through the door. She turned to Margretha. "Here is a stew for you to take home for a meal."

A look of surprise crossed Aunt Margretha's face. "You don't have to do this, Maeyken."

"Yes, I do." She placed a hand on Betteken's shoulder. "And I want to visit your mother in prison too, child. If you'd like to write her a letter, I'll take it with me."[1]

Betteken stared at her. "You would take a letter to Mama for me? Really?"

Mrs. Wils smiled gently. "She'd be glad to hear from you. And I have no doubt that she'd write back to you."

For the first time in hours, excitement leaped into Betteken's eyes. "Oh, thank you!" she cried, throwing her arms around her friend's mother. "Thank you so much!"

---

[1] The *Martyrs Mirror* mentions a woman named Maeyken Wils who took letters to Maeyken Wens in prison.

Maeyken's eyes were wet with tears as she returned Betteken's hug. "I'm glad to do it. And I hope that someday your mother will come home again."

. . . .

Betteken sat at the table, her brow furrowed as she stared down at the paper before her. "I have no idea how to finish this letter, Aunt Margretha."

"What have you written so far?" Margretha stepped up behind her.

"I told her about the new job Father and Adriaen started working on, and how you're here helping us. But I can't think of how to finish it." Betteken glanced up. "Do you have any ideas?"

"Hmm . . ." Margretha slowly wiped another dish with her linen towel and placed it on the shelf with the other pots and kettles. "I'm sure she'd be happy to hear that you pray for her every day."

Betteken dropped her eyes. "I suppose I could tell her that."

Even she could hear the doubt in her voice. Behind her, Aunt Margretha stopped wiping dishes. Betteken bent her head over the paper, feeling the heat creep into her face.

"What's wrong, Betteken?" Aunt Margretha asked softly at length.

"Adriaen doesn't know if praying does any good." She avoided her aunt's eyes as she spoke.

"Really?" Aunt Margretha sat down across from her. "Why does he question that?"

Betteken looked up. "He can't understand why God allowed this to happen."

"And what do you think?"

"I . . ." She hesitated. "I wonder the same thing."

Aunt Margretha sighed a little. "Those are heavy questions for a young girl. But believe me when I say that we really don't have to understand. It's enough to know that God is in control."

Betteken looked down at her paper again as Aunt Margretha stood up. Now she knew how she could end her letter.

Mama, I don't know why God allowed you to be captured and taken to prison, but I want to believe that He is in control. I pray for you every day.

Love, Betteken

She gave the letter to Father that night when he came in for supper. He read it slowly, and when he looked up, there were tears in his eyes. "It's a very nice letter, Betty," he said softly, his voice cracking. "Mama will appreciate it very much."

That night Adriaen also wrote a letter for his mother, but he didn't show it to anyone. Betteken only knew that the next morning when Father left, he took both of their letters, as well as his own, along with him.

. . . .

Rain slashed against window shutters and pelted Antwerp's cobblestone streets. Betteken pulled her hood over her head, squinting in the force of wind and rain as Father stopped in front of her. Adriaen, with Hans in his arms, stepped up beside Betteken.

Reaching out, Father knocked three times. A signal. Moments later the door opened, and Maritgen's father beckoned to them from inside. "Hurry," he whispered. Holding up a candle, he led the way to the parlor.

The other believers were gathered there, standing or sitting on benches along the walls. The room was quiet, and

Betteken instantly felt the tension in the air. They were all remembering their last meeting and wondering if they would be discovered again this time.

When Father began to speak, Betteken could see that it was a struggle for him. Tears glistened in his eyes, and he stopped often to blow his nose. "Friends, we are gathered tonight to pray. Our flesh is weak, and we need faith to withstand this trial. Several of our number are in prison . . ." His voice broke, and he had to stop. Finally he continued, "My dear wife has been taken, and there are others here who have family members in prison as well. Let us lift each other up with prayer so that we might be strong."

There wasn't a dry eye in the room when he finished speaking. It was several minutes before anyone spoke. Then, one by one, the believers prayed aloud.

From the back of the room, a young woman came forward. Her face was tear-stained, but there was confidence in the tilt of her head. Mattheus stepped over to meet her. "What is your need today?"

"I was critical of my sister Janneken and her husband Hans when they first became believers," she said softly. "But I soon saw that they had something different. And I see it in all of you as well. I want it too."

Betteken watched as Father prayed with Grietge Straten at the front of the room. When the young woman rose from her knees, her eyes were shining through her tears. Betteken knew she had found what she was looking for.

Others came forward, confessing doubts and unbelief in

God's power. The room became a holy place as hope and trust took the place of despair.

When they were safely at home again, Betteken asked Father, "What do you think Janneken's father will say when he finds out what is happening to his children?"

Her father thought for a moment. "He will probably be angry," he said finally. "But you don't need to worry about it. Just pray, all right?"

Betteken nodded and fell silent. Did praying truly work? She decided to ask Father. "It seems that no matter how much we pray, nothing changes. Why do we even pray? Does God hear us?"

"Yes, my daughter, God does hear us. But He doesn't always answer the way we want Him to." Mattheus paused. "Praying is vital to the Christian, Betty. It's how we get the strength and courage to go on. God hears us every time we pray. And He always answers, even though we may not see the results right away. His wisdom is beyond ours, and we dare not make Him so small in our minds as to expect to understand everything about how He works."

Betteken hesitated. "I've been praying that Mama will come home again," she said finally. "Will God let it happen?"

"God will do what He sees best, Betty," Father answered kindly. "He may allow all of us to suffer, but He will always be with us through our pain, and He will bring good out of it in the end."

Betteken's throat tightened. She didn't ask any more questions.

CHAPTER ELEVEN

A Trip to Rotterdam

*I*t had been three weeks now since Mama had been taken to prison. Three long, long weeks. Betteken found that life did go on, even without her mother. Aunt Margretha came every day, and her presence cheered them all. She was teaching Betteken how to cook and how to spin thread with Mama's spinning wheel. Betteken didn't know what she would have done without Aunt Margretha.

But there was a hole in their family that was never filled. Hans clung to Aunt Margretha when she was there, and when she left in the evening, he was Betteken's shadow. Adriaen had become quieter, and Father didn't smile as much. Betteken knew he was still praying about decisions they would have to make in the near future.

Betteken had replayed the night of capture over and over in her mind. She felt a burning anger toward the soldiers who had swooped down on their meeting and taken the five prisoners away. It made her feel tight and ugly inside, but she felt she couldn't help it.

Father shook his head when she told him how she felt. "You must forgive them, Betty. They were only following the king's orders, and didn't know what they were doing."

He paused before drawing a folded sheet of paper from his pocket. "Maeyken Wils gave me something today that will interest you very much."

Betteken looked at him questioningly. Then her eyes fell on the script that covered the paper in his hand. "Mama wrote a letter?" she cried, jumping up.

Father laughed. "I'll read it right now. Here, Hans, let me hold you."

> *Grace and peace from God the Father, through Jesus Christ His only begotten Son. I am still tolerably well and trust I'm doing my best, but my best is nothing special. I regret that I'm not more thankful for all that has come upon me. Oh, that I could always thank the Lord when the flesh suffers as well as when it prospers.*[1]

Betteken sat down again at the hearth, and Adriaen joined her. She listened breathlessly as Father began reading again, his voice soft in the stillness of the room.

> *I should never have thought that parting should come so hard to me as it does. True, the*

---
[1] All the letters of Maeyken Wens are found on pages 981–983 in the *Martyrs Mirror*.

imprisonment seemed hard to me, but that was because they were so tyrannical. But now the parting is hardest of all.

Oh, my dear husband, pray that God will remove this conflict from me. It's in His power, if it is His pleasure. Truly the Lord has said, 'He that does not forsake everything is not worthy of me,' for He well knew that this would come hard. But I hope the Lord will help me through as He has helped others. I can simply trust Him.

"Are you going to visit her again?" Adriaen asked when Father fell silent.

"I hope I can," Father said slowly. "But she asks me not to bring anything if I do, because it costs so much."

Betteken went to bed that night feeling happier than she had in weeks. It was so good to hear from Mama again. If only she could be here with them!

The next day, Mattheus was asked to travel to Rotterdam for a secret meeting with other Dutch Anabaptists. Betteken heard him talking about it with the elderly minister, Jan de Metser, that night when he stopped in for a visit. "I hate to go right now with Maeyken in prison," Father said. "And the children . . ." His voice trailed off.

Jan was silent for a moment, thinking. "It wouldn't take longer than a few days," he said at last. "If anything happens to Maeyken while you are gone, God will make sure you find out in His perfect timing."

After Jan left, Adriaen stepped close to Father. "I want to go along."

Father looked at him for a long moment. "It's dangerous to go," he warned.

Adriaen shrugged. "It's dangerous here too."

Betteken sat quietly at the fireplace, listening. Hans stood beside her, his blue eyes serious as he looked from Father to Adriaen. Father glanced toward them. "I could ask your grandparents if they can take you in while we're gone," he said slowly.

"Father," Betteken spoke up. "I want to go too."

He shook his head. "No, Betty. Hans needs you here."

"But, Father," she said, tears welling up in her eyes. "If you and Adriaen go and get caught—" She choked to a stop. "Please," she whispered. "I can't bear to be away from you."

"Betteken." Father's voice was exceedingly kind. "I can't allow you to go along. It's too dangerous. But you can pray for us while we're gone." Tipping her chin, he looked deep in her eyes. "I need you to be strong, daughter. Your prayers help me more than you know."

She swallowed hard and finally nodded. "All right, Father," she whispered. "I'll stay home. And I'll pray for you the whole time you're gone."

. . . .

The day that he was to leave with Father, Adriaen awoke with a feeling of excitement that outweighed his fear.

Normally he stayed home with Mama and the others when Father went on a journey. He dressed quickly and was running a hand through his blond hair when he heard a knock on the door below.

He stepped to his open bedroom door as the low murmur of voices reached his ears. Adriaen recognized Father's, but he couldn't discern the other voice. He couldn't understand what they were saying, either. Concern swept over him. What was happening?

But there was laughter in Father's tone when he called up the stairs seconds later. "Come and see what Maeyken Wils brought for us this morning!"

Betteken flew out of her room, nearly colliding with Adriaen at the top of the stairs. They raced down to the kitchen where Father waited, his eyes shining. "There's a letter from Mama. It's for both of you."

Adriaen opened the letter with care. Mama's dainty script filled both sides of the paper, and his throat constricted just to see it. Pulling up a chair, he spread it out on the table before him.

> *Adriaen, my son, because you are the oldest, I exhort you that you should begin to fear our dear Lord. You're getting old enough to perceive what is good or evil. Think of Betteken, who is about as old as you are. My son, follow that which is good and depart from evil. Do good while you have time. Watch your father*

and note how lovingly he treated me with kindness and courteousness, always instructing me with the Word of the Lord.

Look at the little flock, persecuted for their faith. The good persecute none, but are persecuted. When you have joined them, beware of all false doctrine, for John says: 'Whosoever transgresseth, and abideth not in the doctrine of Christ, hath not God. He that abideth in the doctrine of Christ, he hath both the Father and the Son.' The doctrine of Christ is mercy, peace, purity, faith, meekness, humbleness, and full obedience to God.

My dear son, yield yourself to that which is good; the Lord will give you understanding. Heed the Lord's chastening, for whenever you do evil, He will chasten you in your mind. God the Father, through His beloved Son Jesus Christ, grant you His Holy Spirit, that He may guide you into all truth.

Write me a letter as to what your heart says, whether you desire to fear the Lord; this I should like to know. But you must write it better than the last two letters were written.

Adriaen could almost see Mama smiling as she wrote those words.

The one which Maeyken Wils brought, however, was good.

Adriaen read the last paragraph twice before slowly folding the letter again. When he looked up, Betteken was standing behind him. "Are you going to answer her question?"

He didn't answer for a long moment. "After I go to Rotterdam . . ." He glanced toward Father. "Perhaps I will then."

. . . .

The cart Mattheus borrowed from one of the church brethren had seats for two. While his son steered the horse, Mattheus studied, always carefully concealing his Bible as they rode through the streets. He didn't want to raise anybody's suspicions.

Dusk was falling by the time they reached Rotterdam. The city was near the sea, with ships sailing in and out of its port. The waves were tossed by the strong winds of an approaching storm.

The secret meeting was held in a house within the city. Adriaen stood at the back of the room, watching silently as Father read from the Scriptures. Three people had asked for baptism this night: a boy and two girls, all near his own age.

Adriaen knew that one of the girls was Lucia Willemsdochter.[2]

---

[2] The Dutch did not have "last names" the way we have. Rather, their surnames were their father's names. Dirk's full last name was Willemszoon, "son of Willem." Lucia's full last name, Willemsdochter, means "daughter of Willem."

He had heard a story about her brother Dirk Willems, who had been persecuted for his faith. As he was running from the authorities who were trying to capture him, he crossed a frozen river. The man who was following him most closely fell through the ice. When he called for help, Dirk decided to turn back and rescue him. The grateful man had wanted to let Dirk go free, but he was persuaded by the others to keep him in bondage. So Dirk had been taken back to prison, where he was later killed for his faith.[3]

That had happened four years ago. Now Dirk's sister Lucia was getting baptized. Reddish hair framed her sweet face, and her dark eyes held a serious look. Two younger girls and a woman with silvery hair stood with her. Adriaen wondered if they were Lucia's mother and sisters.

Though Adriaen had heard the baptismal questions many times before, never had they struck him as deeply as now. "Have you repented of all your sins, and are you willing to crucify your sinful body with Christ, and die to sin? Do you promise by the grace of God to submit yourself unto Christ and faithfully serve Him until death?"

Write me a letter as to what your heart says, whether you desire to fear the Lord; this I should like to know, his mother had written. Adriaen knew that he could give her no greater joy than to know that he had decided to follow Christ. Something else in her letter came to his mind. *The doctrine of Christ is mercy, peace, purity, faith, meekness, humbleness,*

---

[3] The story of Dirk Willems is found on pages 741–742 in the *Martyrs Mirror*.

and full obedience to God. Was he ready for all it meant to be a true Christian?

His father was glancing around the circle now. "Does anyone else desire to repent of your sins tonight? Believe on Jesus Christ and enter the kingdom of peace."

Adriaen took a step forward, but then hesitated. *God is supposed to be loving and kind,* a voice whispered. *If that's true, why does He allow things like this to happen? Your mother is in prison. Your father is in danger. Where is His mercy in it all?*

Confusion rose anew, and he stopped, watching as Father began to baptize the young people. He simply couldn't do it. Not yet.

Some people left immediately after the meeting, but others stayed a little longer to talk. "We appreciate you coming, Brother Mattheus," one man said. "We heard that your wife is in prison."

Father nodded. "I have a daughter and three year-old son at home, as well as my son Adriaen who came with me."

"Some among us are in prison as well," Lucia's mother spoke up. "I am encouraged to see young people experience the new birth in these perilous times."

As the gathering broke up, one man lingered. "You are welcome to come to my home for the night," he offered.

Father shook his head. "Thank you, but we want to get back as soon as possible."

"I understand, brother," he answered quietly. "Go, and God be with you."

"Son, I saw you start forward, but then you stopped." Mattheus spoke in a whisper as he flicked the reins, steering the horse around a curve in the trees. "Why?"

Adriaen felt the heat rise in his face. "I want to give my life to Christ someday, Father," he said miserably, "but I'm so confused. I just don't understand how God can love us and allow all these bad things to happen. We need Mama, and she's in prison!"

His father looked thoughtful. "God's ways are beyond our understanding. Sometimes He allows trials to make us stronger. We have to simply trust that God knows what He is doing."

He glanced around. "We must be careful. Sometimes the forest itself seems to have ears."

Adriaen followed his gaze toward a grove of trees. Deep shadows hung there, able to conceal anyone who wished to remain hidden. They didn't speak again until they were near the deserted road. "Father, I don't know if I could bear it if you were captured," Adriaen said at last.

Mattheus glanced at him. "Whatever happens to me is in God's hands, son. We need to simply trust Him."

Adriaen looked away without replying.

CHAPTER TWELVE

"You Must Forgive"

Betteken sat on a stool, watching Adriaen as he brushed down Father's horse in the stall. "I'm more confused than ever," he confessed. "I want to believe, to experience the joy those people do. But the truth is, I just can't understand how God works. If He truly loved us . . ." His voice trailed off.

"Are you going to write to Mama about this?" she asked softly.

He shook his head. "It would only hurt her, Betteken. And she's going through enough right now."

Stars were twinkling high overhead when they closed the barn door and started for the house. The windows were open, and Betteken could see Father sitting in his chair by the fire, rocking Hans. Her little brother hadn't let Father out of his sight since he'd come home.

After washing her hands, Betteken sat down at the spinning wheel. She fastened the fibers of wool to the distaff as Aunt Margretha had taught her, but her fingers fumbled and the wool blurred before her eyes. If only it were Mama spinning before the fire! The ache in Betteken's heart deepened.

Slowly she began spinning. For a moment, the only sound in the room was the soft thumping of the spinning wheel. From time to time, Betteken watched her father. He was quiet tonight, and the look in his eyes made her heart ache. Mama had always been there before to meet him when he came home from a trip. She had no doubt that he missed Mama even more than they did.

Slipping from her seat, she went to him. "Father?"

She felt better when he smiled and gave her a hug. Then he took the sleeping Hans into his bedroom and closed the door. He didn't come back out again.

. . . .

Spring had come.

These days the sun shone warmly, and housewives adorned their window shutters with baskets of flowers. Their fragrance scented the balmy breezes. Betteken and Hans went to the fields and forests beyond the city gates to gather flowers for their own basket. The colors were so bright and cheerful that Betteken wished her own life could be like that—only flowers, sunshine, and laughter, with no trouble hanging over it.

"You can live in a world like that someday," Father said when she told him of her wish. "Heaven is a wonderful place, full of happiness and beauty. There's no sin in it whatsoever." Betteken could hardly imagine it.

Elizabeth was free to roam with her now, completely well

······················ "YOU MUST FORGIVE"

again. To Betteken she seemed like the soul of spring—carefree and laughing, scattering sunbeams wherever she went. Maritgen often joined them too. The three girls spent hours together.

One rainy night in May, Elizabeth and her mother attended a meeting for the first time. "Mama may ask for baptism soon," Elizabeth told Betteken as they gathered nuts in the woods the next day.

"How do you feel about that?"

Elizabeth smiled. "I'm proud of her. Your people are unusual. Even in the midst of all the struggles you face, your faith just grows stronger."

Troubled at heart, Betteken wasn't sure how to answer. That night she told Adriaen, "I knew deep inside that Elizabeth wasn't talking about me when she said 'your people.' Whenever I remember those soldiers, I get angry all over again."

Her brother stiffened. "I don't want to talk about it," he said shortly.

Standing up, he left the room. Betteken watched him go in silence. Then she turned to her father, who was sitting near the fire. The sadness in his eyes made her hesitate. Yet she had to ask.

"Father, do you ever struggle to forgive the soldiers for capturing Mama?"

His eyes shadowed. "I often pray that God will help me love them with His love. They have souls just like you and me, Betteken. And God loves them just as much as He loves us."

"That's hard to believe," she mumbled, even as she felt shame creep into her heart.

"But it's true." Father leaned forward. "Betteken, God loves every one of those people who persecute us. He doesn't want anyone to go to hell at the end of this life. We're called to be a light to them. Do you remember Anthonis Ysbaerts? It was through what he saw at the executions of the believers that he became converted."

He paused. "Like I said before, those soldiers were only doing their duty. When Jesus was dying on the cross, He said, 'Father, forgive them, for they know not what they do.' If Jesus could forgive His persecutors, don't you think we should? He went through more than what we ever will."

"But how can I?" she whispered.

"If you ask, Jesus will help you love them with His love."

The words hung between them, and Betteken fought back a sob. "I do want to forgive, Father. I'm tired of feeling angry all the time."

"Before you go to bed tonight, tell God how you feel," Father encouraged as he stood up. "He wants you to pour out your heart before Him." He reached for a candle and held out his hand to Hans. "Come, little son. It's time for bed."

Betteken left the room without saying anything more. In her room, she knelt down beside her bed, gazing for a moment at the stars shining in the night sky. "Dear God, I want the peace that Father has," she whispered. "But I feel so angry at those soldiers. Don't they have any heart at all? Please help me to forgive and love them with your love . . ."

Her voice trailed off. Deep within, a warm feeling circled her heart. She had never felt anything like it before.

In that moment, she seemed to see again the soldiers charging through the trees, swooping down on their meeting and taking captive the group of five prisoners. But the picture had somehow changed. Instead, she saw their souls, held captive in the darkness of deception. And she knew that she could forgive. God loved each of those soldiers, and He would help her love them too.

CHAPTER THIRTEEN

Janneken's Baby

Market day was always crowded. People filled the streets, setting up tables with items to sell. Betteken hurried down the sidewalk, dodging between tables as the gusty summer wind painted a flush of color in her cheeks. She heard someone shout angrily at her but kept on going, intent on getting home as quickly as possible.

"You! Girl!"

The shout came again, and this time Betteken stopped. Turning, she faced an elderly man standing behind her. Loaves of bread were scattered in the street, and his eyes glared. "Watch where you're going!" he sputtered, pointing at the bread. "You clean this up, and no running off till you're finished."

Betteken glanced anxiously at his face and nodded. "I'm sorry, sir," she said politely. "I'll clean it up right away."

He watched her for a moment, and Betteken felt uncomfortable under his stare. She didn't look up as the man spoke again. "You're the daughter of Mattheus Wens, aren't you?"

Betteken paled and stood up, placing the last loaf of bread on the table. "I have to go," she murmured, turning to leave.

Two tables away, she stopped and glanced back. The elderly man was helping someone else now, and she took the chance to melt into the crowd. She didn't want him to see her again.

Breaking into a run, Betteken passed the stone cathedral and turned into her home street. Here again she had to dodge tables and people. All the while, the words pounded in her head: *I have to find him! I have to find him!*

"I heard my uncle talking with Mama last night," Elizabeth had told her. "She was trying to reason with him, saying that it's nothing but cruelty to capture and kill your people. But he says that all treason must be punished, and he's determined to mete out justice. He said that if they'd find all the leaders, perhaps they could stop the Anabaptist heresy from spreading." Elizabeth's voice dropped. "Betteken, I heard him say that the soldiers will arrest your father today."

Betteken didn't wait for Elizabeth to say more. Bidding her friend a hasty goodbye, she dashed out the door. And now she was racing down her home street toward the small stone house near the city gates. Was Father at home? She didn't let herself think about what would happen if she couldn't find him.

Bursting through the door, she slammed it shut and leaned against it for a moment, panting. The kitchen was empty, and she hurried into the next room. No one was there either.

"Father!" she shouted. "Father, are you here?"

Fear seized her. Had the soldiers captured Father already?

"Father," she cried again. "Please answer!"

Silence. Betteken stood there, shaking. Outside she could hear the clamor of people and animals in the street. Where was Father? Adriaen and Hans had also gone into the streets, but Father had said that he was going to stay home to fast and pray.

A small sound at the doorway of the parlor made her turn. There stood Father, his eyes serious. "Betty, what's wrong? Why are you so afraid?"

Betteken released her breath and willed herself to speak sensibly. "Father, you must hide right away." Her voice trembled. "The soldiers are coming to find you. Elizabeth told me."

"Are you sure?"

"She heard Father Wils say so."

Father sighed. "Then . . . I suppose I'll have to go. Betteken, listen to me. Find your brothers and tell Adriaen about this. And ask Aunt Margretha to stay here with you while I'm gone."

Betteken followed him to his room, where he quickly packed a small bundle. Stepping to the door, he turned back. "Don't worry about me, Betteken. Remember to pray. God is with me and I'm in His care, no matter what happens."

After giving her a quick hug, he opened the door and strode into the street. Betteken watched from the window until he disappeared.

. . . .

The days in the cell stretched on and on. Nights seemed even longer as Maeyken Wens lay awake, thinking unceasingly of her family. The time she spent quoting Bible verses to herself helped to keep up her courage.

At times, the guards took her to the courtroom to be questioned. Even when they tortured her, she would not recant. Christ had done so much for her, and she wanted to give her all to Him in return.

Her fellow prisoners had been placed in other cells now. She had no idea what was happening to them. She could do nothing but wait and pray.

. . . .

The Scheldt River rippled and sparkled, reflecting the crystal blue color of the September sky. From where they stood on the shore, Betteken and Aunt Margretha could watch the waves crashing against the rocks and the ships sailing into harbor. Betteken sighed. "I wish Mama could see this . . ." she breathed wistfully.

Her aunt's eyes softened as she clasped Betteken's hand. "Maybe someday she will be with you again."

"I wish so much that life could be the way it used to be." But Betteken didn't voice all her thoughts. Public places, even this peaceful spot, held a threat of discovery if she were to mention that her father was in hiding.

Even though it had happened several months ago, the day the soldiers came for Father was still vivid in her mind. They had marched down the street, their swords flashing in the sunlight. Aunt Margretha had glanced out the window before speaking quickly to Betteken, "Stay close to me." She picked up Hans as a forceful knock sounded on the door.

Aunt Margretha's face was calm when she opened it. "May I help you, sir?"

The tall officer's eyes seemed to take in everything. A scar across his left cheek made him look well-seasoned in his work. "We have come in the king's name with a warrant for the arrest of the heretic minister, Mattheus Wens."

Aunt Margretha did not respond. Instead, she stepped through the door, leaving it open. Betteken followed close behind. They stood against the side of the house, waiting without speaking as the soldiers clomped inside. Betteken wondered how many people were watching. Their family secrets would shortly be known throughout the city.

It seemed like hours before the soldiers finally came back out. The leading officer wore a dark scowl, and his tone was ominous as he spoke a last word to Aunt Margretha. "We're keeping our eyes on you. We're not resting until we find Mattheus Wens!"

Ever since that day, neighbors had whispered in little groups on street corners, watching them with guarded stares. Betteken often saw sentries stroll slowly by their house. She felt intensely relieved that Father was in hiding, but it didn't alleviate the pain of rejection from society. Maritgen, Elizabeth, and Elizabeth's mother remained among their few faithful friends. Life slowly settled into a routine. But Betteken wondered if the gaping wound in her heart would ever heal.

"Betteken?" Hans tugged at her hand. "Let's race home!"

Shaking off the troubling memories, Betteken smiled down at him. "Okay, little brother. Are you ready?" Hans nodded eagerly, and she counted, "One, two, three, go!"

Shouting with laughter, Hans raced ahead. Betteken laughed too and took care to stay behind him. Hans would be absolutely thrilled if he won.

The wind caught Betteken's skirt, making it swirl around her. Her cap slipped back over her head, letting strands of blond hair escape from her coiled braid. As they rounded a corner in the street, Betteken stopped short, and the laughter died on her lips.

Turning abruptly, Hans ran back to her. She caught him up and stood frozen in place, watching soldiers lead Hans Munstdorp through the prison gates. Fear clutched her chest so that she could hardly breathe.

The day Johannes the printer had been burned flashed vividly into her mind. She had no doubt that these soldiers were leading Hans to his death. Would he be burned too?

Frantic now, she glanced toward the prison. Was Hans Munstdorp the only one who'd been sentenced to death?

Just then she felt a hand on her shoulder. "Come, Betteken," Aunt Margretha said softly in her ear. "Let's go."

She couldn't speak, but Aunt Margretha read the question in her eyes. "It's just Hans today. The others are still in prison."[1]

Betteken swallowed hard. "It's been five months now," she

---
[1] Hans Munstdorp was burned to death in September 1573.

said hoarsely. "What will happen to the others? Will they let them come home after Hans is killed?"

Aunt Margretha could only shake her head and answer, "I don't know, Betty. I don't know."

. . . .

Betteken worked beside Aunt Margretha, helping her make supper. Normally the *sluberkens,* their crusts stuffed with marrow, sugar, currants, and cinnamon, would have made her mouth water. But tonight she had no appetite at all.

Aunt Margretha seemed to move more slowly too. The sparkle in her dark eyes was gone, and she often stopped in her work to stare out the window.

The rattle of the latch on the gate broke the heavy silence. "Is that Adriaen?" Betteken asked.

Aunt Margretha glanced out the window. "Why, it's Grietge Straten. I wonder if she has news . . ." Her voice trailed off. Quickly washing her hands, she opened the door. "Grietge!"

"Margretha, I had to come see you." The young woman's face was tear-stained, and her lips trembled.

"Please come in." Aunt Margretha turned to Betteken. "Will you go see what Hans is doing? He's outside."

Betteken knew that was her way of saying that she wanted to speak with Grietge alone. She nodded and hurried to the door.

Hans was playing on the steps, his blond hair shining in the sunset's last light. Betteken stood looking down at him, her heart swelling. How she loved her little brother! It seemed simply cruel that men had torn his mother away from him.

She worried about her father as well. Even if he was hiding, he wasn't really safe.

The verse in Psalms came again to her mind: *The Lord is my light . . . whom shall I fear?* Betteken thought of those words now as she watched her little brother. Her parents said that God was with them, and there was nothing to fear. She wanted to believe it, but it was hard.

The door behind her opened, and Grietge came out. She seemed more relaxed now, and stopped to pat Hans's head. When she was gone, Betteken went back into the kitchen. "What did she want, Aunt Margretha?"

There was a hint of tears in her aunt's eyes. "Oh, Betteken. We must pray for them."

"Pray for who? What are you talking about?"

"Grietge has a little niece." Aunt Margretha stopped and drew a breath. "The reason it's taken so long for the prisoners to be sentenced is because the authorities were waiting until Janneken's baby was born."[2]

Betteken gasped. "Janneken had a baby?"

"Yes, she was carrying the baby before she was captured, but not many people knew about it. The little girl was born about a week ago." A tender smile flickered over Aunt Margretha's face. "Grietge smuggled the baby out of prison. Janneken wanted her child to go to her friends as soon as possible. She is now in the hands of a young couple from our congregation, and they will raise the baby as their own daughter." She paused. "Grietge said that Janneken thinks

---

[2] Janneken's story is found on pages 983–991 in the *Martyrs Mirror*.

her life is nearly over, and she doesn't want the priests to find her baby. They wouldn't allow her to grow up among our people if they did."

"What is the baby's name?" Betteken asked softly. "Will I ever get to see her?"

"Perhaps someday. She is named Janneken, after her mother."

One day the next week Betteken saw a horse-drawn wagon coming down the street. Grietge and a young couple she had often seen at Anabaptist meetings were riding in it. In her arms, Grietge held a tiny baby wrapped in a woolen cloth. She smiled and waved as they passed by.

Betteken stood still for a long moment, looking after them. She would never forget this tiny baby who had been born in prison to a mother who chose to give her up rather than recanting her faith so she could raise her daughter herself. She had given her child to friends who would love her and teach her the way of Christ. By doing this, Janneken Munstdorp had shown her baby the truest kind of love.

CHAPTER FOURTEEN

The Trial

Early October breezes chilled Betteken's arms as she swished her hand through the soapy water. Aunt Margretha worked nearby, laying clothes out to dry. Betteken finished her load of laundry and sat back.

Fall was a season she had always loved. The weather made her think of bygone days, unlocking the door to beautiful memories. But this year was different. Mama was in prison and Father was gone, hiding from authorities. She didn't know where he was. Thinking of how her life used to be brought such deep pain that she had to force the memories away.

"Betteken?"

Marıtgen's voice broke into her reverie, and Betteken turned sharply. "Where did you come from?" she exclaimed in surprise.

Her friend laughed. "I thought you looked far away. What were you thinking about?"

"I asked you a question first," laughed Betteken.

"I had to run a few errands for Mama, and thought I'd come

see you." Maritgen paused. "I just wanted you to know that I'm praying for you while both your mother and father are gone." Maritgen spoke so quietly that Betteken had to lean forward to hear. "I know it must be hard."

Betteken felt a lump come into her throat. "Thanks, Maritgen."

"Mama sent some gingerbread for you. Shall I take it to the house?"

"I'll go in with you," Aunt Margretha said, standing up.

Betteken turned back to her work as Maritgen and Aunt Margretha left. A solitary tear dripped into the water.

"We must be brave," Adriaen had told her. "For Hans's sake, as much as our own." She knew he was right and promised to do her best. In the daylight it wasn't as hard. Then she was always busy, helping with the housework or shopping for food with Aunt Margretha.

But at night when she was alone, Betteken often cried herself to sleep.

. . . .

Adriaen was leaving the marketplace when he saw the crowd of people gathering in the courtyard. He stopped an older man hurrying by. "What's going on?"

"They're finally taking those heretics to trial!" The hard glint in the man's eyes made Adriaen stiffen with fear. He stood still for a moment before rushing after the man.

The courtroom was already packed, with people standing along the walls and filling the balcony. Adriaen hurried up the steps to the balcony, choosing a place where he could clearly see everything that went on below.

Seven judges were seated behind the desk, solemn and imposing. One raised his hand for silence. "Guards, bring Janneken Munstdorp into the room."

Two guards left the room and quickly returned with the young woman. The courtroom was completely silent as she came forward, erect and calm.

"You have been charged with heresy," the judge began, his eyes on the parchment in his hand. "You refuse to claim membership with the state church, and have been re-baptized. Is this true?"

"It is true."

"The penalty for this is death." He glanced up, his voice softening. "Think of what this means. You have a newborn daughter. A mother should be at home to care for her child."

Janneken did not flinch. "You should take good heed," she said. "Our blood will be severely required at your hands."

One of the other judges leaned forward. "We did not do it. It was the decree of the king."

"This will not save you," she answered. "The Lord would forgive you if you did it ignorantly, but I think that you know well enough what kind of people we are."

"We wash our hands from this." Color flushed the judge's neck.

"Pilate did so too," she said quietly.

His head jerked up, and sparks shot from his eyes. "Pilate was a just judge. You acted contrary to the king's command!"

"We have greater reason to obey God than the king." Janneken was still calm. "It is a little matter that you sentence us to death, because we don't know how long we'll live, but we know that we must certainly die sometime. You should take caution with the shedding of innocent blood."

"Innocent blood!" he roared, leaping to his feet. "You committed treason against the state church! According to the law, you are guilty! You deserve to die!"

This time, Janneken made no answer. The rest of the room erupted as the people called for justice. The other three women were quickly brought forward for questioning, but there was hardly any need. The decision was made, and the sentences quickly passed. The four women—Janneken Munstdorp, Maeyken Wens, Mariken, and Lijsken—would be burned to death on the next day, the sixth of October.

After the women had been taken back to prison, Adriaen got to his feet and shoved through the crowd, desperate to get home. The day had taken on a nightmarish quality, but the growing lump in his throat and the sting in his eyes were all too real. It had been so good to see his mother again, even though the six months in prison had changed her. She was thinner now, and her face was gaunt. But her clear blue eyes still held the same serenity. She was sure of her destiny, and there was no turning back.

If I could only talk with her one more time. Just once more. But he knew it was impossible. As he opened the gate to their house, his legs seemed to give way. He sank to the ground and, dropping his head into his hands, allowed grief to overtake him.

. . . .

THE TRIAL

Moonlight slanted through the small window of the cell. Maeyken Wens sat on the cold stone floor below it, writing the last letter she would ever write to her son. Silent tears trickled down her cheeks, making it hard to see in the dim lighting.

Oh, my dear son, though I am taken from you here, strive to fear God, and you will have your

mother again in the New Jerusalem, where parting will be no more. My dear son, I hope now to go before you; follow me as much as you value your soul, for there is no other way to salvation. I will commend you to the Lord; may He keep you. I trust the Lord that He will do it, if you seek Him. Love one another all the days of your life; take care of Hansken for me. And if your father should be taken from you, care for your siblings. The Lord keep you, one and all.

My dear son, don't be afraid of this suffering. It is nothing compared to that which will endure forever. The Lord takes away all fear; I felt joy when I was sentenced. I cannot fully thank my God for the great grace which He has shown me. Adieu once more, my dear son Adriaen; always be kind to your afflicted father, and do not grieve him. This letter is addressed to you, but I mean for you to share it with all of my children. With that, I commend you to the Lord once more.

Maeyken read over the letter twice and then slowly folded it. Bowing her head, she prayed that the letter would bless and encourage her son.

CHAPTER FIFTEEN

Memorial in the Ashes

The great fireball of the sun edged eastern clouds with gold. As she braided her long hair, Betteken felt a tight feeling of dread in her stomach. How she wished that she could go back to bed and sleep until this day was over.

Last evening Adriaen had told them of the trial and death sentences. Turning, she stepped to the window. From here she couldn't see the prison, but she could imagine her mother praying in her cell. Pulling on her linen cap, she slipped to her knees beside the bed. "Dear Lord," she whispered. "Please help us through this day!"

Aunt Margretha was in the kitchen, preparing breakfast. When Betteken came to stand beside her, she gave her niece a hug. "Could you sleep at all last night, Betteken?" she asked.

Betteken nodded, not trusting herself to speak. Her aunt smoothed back her hair and spoke softly. "Will you set up the table, please?"

Betteken nodded again and moved toward the wall where

123

the round table was kept. She unfolded it and spread a tablecloth over top. The familiar task was comforting. Even though her world was torn apart, some things hadn't changed.

Adriaen came into the kitchen, his face pale and determined. He stopped beside Betteken and spoke quietly. "I'm going to watch the proceedings today. Do you want to come along?"

She shook her head mutely.

"I'll take Hans with me," he went on. "You won't have to worry about taking care of him all day."

Betteken's pain deepened. Dear little Hans would hardly remember his mother when he grew older.

Aunt Margretha's prayer that morning brought a measure of solace to her heart. "Heavenly Father, we're thankful that you care about what we are facing. Please keep us all safe in your loving care. May we submit to your will today. Grant us your peace . . ."

. . . .

Adriaen held Hans tightly as he walked down the street, heading toward the town square near the prison. Already a crowd had gathered, thronging the street as the guards led their prisoners toward the gates. As the four chained women drew near the execution site, they said nothing, but simply watched the crowd. Adriaen saw his mother walking with a guard on either side of her. Her blue eyes were searching the crowd, and he hoped against hope that she would see him. But he could hardly even see her now because of the tears blinding his eyes.

The October day was cold, and Hans shivered in Adriaen's arms, his wide blue eyes darting here and there. Adriaen wondered if he recognized his mother at all. Probably not—it had been six months since he'd last seen her.

Four stakes had been set up in the square, and the guards were already piling wood for the fire. Spotting a bench nearby, Adriaen hurried toward it. From there he'd be standing above the press of the crowd and could clearly see what was going on.

Hans squirmed in his arms, and he set the small boy down. Brushing away tears, he glanced back toward his mother. Her clear gaze locked with his, and he knew then that she had seen him. Joy flooded his heart. He smiled in response, wishing he could wave to her. But he didn't dare. The authorities had been known to arrest people in the crowd who tried to encourage the prisoners.

The soldiers worked quickly, fastening their prisoners to the stakes. When they stepped back, the executioner came forward with a torch in his hand. Adriaen felt his legs go weak as flames began shooting up from the wood around the stakes. The crackling of the fire seared his senses, filling him with horror at what he was seeing. He swayed, only vaguely aware of falling to the ground. Then he knew nothing more.

. . . .

Adriaen stirred, his eyes opening slowly. Where was he? Why was he lying on the ground?

A small hand touched his face. "Get up," someone was saying over and over. "Adriaen, get up!"

As if in a dream, he recognized Hans's voice. Still confused, he sat up. "Hans?" His brother's frightened eyes spilled over with tears. The acrid scent of smoke filled the air, and Adriaen felt a wave of dizziness hit him again. It was all coming back to him now.

"I'm all right, Hans." He held out his arms, and Hans ran into them. Adriaen stood up slowly and glanced back toward the square where the execution had taken place. The crowds were gone, and the ashes held no more life.

The deed was done. All those months of waiting and uncertainty about Mama were over. She was gone now, and her soul was in heaven with God and the angels. Adriaen fought back sobs as he moved slowly toward the ashes. He simply couldn't leave without taking a closer look.

He stopped at the burned stake to which his mother had been fastened. His breath caught. *Why not explore the ashes?* If there was anything left, he wanted it as a remembrance of his mother.

Hans waited nearby as Adriaen knelt down to grope through the ashes. He was almost ready to give up when underneath the ashes he felt a hard, oddly-shaped object. He picked it up and turned it over in his hand. A tongue screw.

Sobbing gasps tore through his chest as he stared down at it. This was all that was left of his mother—a tongue screw.

Hans tugged at his arm, bringing Adriaen out of his shock. Slipping the tongue screw into his pocket, he stood up and lifted his brother into his arms. "Come, Hans," he whispered. "Let's go home."

. . . .

Betteken saw her brothers coming. Bursting through the door, she hurried to the gate. "Adriaen?"

His eyes were filled with pain, and she could see that Hans had been crying. Adriaen led the way to the steps and slumped down. "Betteken . . . I didn't see everything. I passed out. But afterward . . ." He stopped and swallowed hard. "I found this."

Reaching into his pocket, he held out the tongue screw. Betteken took it and studied it for a long moment. "Their tongues were screwed so they couldn't talk," Adriaen said quietly. "This is all that was left in the ashes."

Betteken stared at him and then looked down at the tongue screw again. As full reality sank in, she began to weep, her whole body shaking with the force of her sobs.

CHAPTER SIXTEEN

Father's Decision

Night fell gently over the city as stars appeared high in the sky. Betteken stood at the window, gazing into the heavens. "Just think," she murmured. "Mama is somewhere up there right now."

"What do you think she's doing?" Adriaen asked.

A faint smile touched Betteken's lips even as tears threatened. "I think she's rejoicing."

"All of heaven is rejoicing this night," Aunt Margretha said softly. "Four of God's children have arrived safely home."

Someone rapped on the door and opened it. The next instant a cloaked figure stepped inside the house and shut the door quickly. "I was hoping you'd be here," he said with a tremulous smile.

Betteken gasped and jumped to her feet. "Father!" she cried, throwing both arms around him. "Oh, Father! You came back again!"

Mattheus pulled Betteken into his arms, surrounding her with strength. When he let her go, she saw the tears in his eyes. "It's so good to see you, Betty."

"Were you followed?" Aunt Margretha asked urgently, standing up.

"I don't think so." Bending down to pick up the small boy who came running to him, Mattheus asked, "How are you, Hans?"

Hans beamed and patted his father's face with both hands. "I knew you'd come back!"

Mattheus sat down beside Adriaen at the hearth. "It's been a hard day for all of you, hasn't it?"

Adriaen swallowed hard and looked away. "Were you there?" he asked huskily.

"No." Their father shook his head, tears in his own eyes. "But I have something for you, son." Drawing a folded sheet of paper from his pocket, he handed it to Adriaen.

Adriaen took it and stared down at it. "A letter from Mama?" he whispered, barely able to speak.

"She wrote it last night after she was sentenced," Father said softly.

Adriaen's fingers fumbled as he unfolded the paper. Betteken read it over his shoulder, the words blurring as tears misted her eyes. She knew that this was something her brother would treasure forever, even more than the tongue screw.

There was silence for a moment. Then Adriaen looked up. "Father, I know what God is asking me to do, and I want to obey," he said without preamble. "I want to do it right now, while I still have the chance. I may not have tomorrow." He paused. "Life seems very fragile to me now."

Mattheus looked at him keenly. "Are you sure you want to do this after what you witnessed today?"

Adriaen returned his gaze steadily. "There's no question in my mind, Father. I don't understand why God allows things like this to happen, but I believe that He is in control. And I want to submit to Him as Lord of my life."

The words hung between them for a long moment. When Adriaen knelt beside the hearth, Father slipped down beside him. Adriaen's voice was a near whisper as he began to pray. "Dear Lord, I repent of my sins. Please forgive my doubts. I want to submit to you and obey you all of my days."

Betteken stood very still as Adriaen stopped. Then, without making a sound, she stepped over to the hearth and knelt down beside her brother. "Dear God," she said softly, "I repent of my sins too. Please change me and help me find a refuge in you."

There were tears in their father's eyes as he placed his arms around their shoulders. "I have no greater joy than to know that my children walk in truth," he said, smiling through his tears. "God welcomed four of His children home today. And now you have given Him cause for even greater joy."

Adriaen was silent for a long moment. "Do you think Mama knows about what I just decided?" he asked at last.

"She might, son. The Bible says that all of heaven rejoices over one sinner who repents."

Betteken hoped that Mama did indeed know what had just taken place. She glanced into Adriaen's shining eyes and knew that this moment would change their lives forever.

In the silence that followed, Aunt Margretha spoke quietly. "Why did you come back again, Mattheus? Is the danger past?"

Mattheus shook his head, and his face shadowed. "I've made a decision." His voice caught, and his arms tightened around Hans. "Now that my dear wife is gone, we have no reason to stay here. We're leaving Antwerp."

The room became absolutely still. Adriaen was the first to speak, his voice a whisper. "We're leaving?"

"It's too dangerous to stay here any longer, son. I want to move to a place where we can all live together again."

Betteken felt frozen. "Leave?" she whispered. Leave Antwerp, the only home she'd ever known, for a strange place? Leave her friends, her grandparents—Aunt Margretha? "Oh, Father," she murmured, tears welling in her eyes.

Father turned his pain-filled eyes toward her. "I'm afraid this is our only choice if we all want to be together again, Betteken."

She lowered her head and nodded. "I'd rather live with you, even if we have to leave our home," she whispered.

Father sighed a little. "These past months have been hard for all of us."

"Where will we go?" Adriaen asked.

"I want to go to a safer region in Holland. We'll have to leave at night so we won't be seen when we leave the city." He paused before adding, "We'll take tomorrow to get ready for our move and be ready to leave by nightfall."

Betteken felt her throat tighten. *So soon.* But she knew

that Father was right. They wouldn't be able to live together unless they fled this city.

"You'll find a new home in Holland and grow to love it," Aunt Margretha said softly, squeezing Betteken's hand. "Most of all, you'll be safe there—or at least as safe as you can be in these times," she added with a slight smile.

Father took out his Bible, paging carefully through it. "Do you remember the verse I shared with you some time ago, before all this happened to us?" he asked. "I want to share it with you again tonight. 'The LORD is my light and my salvation; whom shall I fear? The LORD is the strength of my life; of whom shall I be afraid?' "

He glanced up. "Let's claim this verse as our promise. When God is on our side, we are safe. No matter what happens, nothing can pluck us from His hand. He is a refuge for our souls."

Betteken knelt down beside her bed that night, her heart swelling with emotion. Mama had often spoken about being safe in God's hand. God did love them, and He would not forsake them. His grace and divine power would lead them safely to their home beyond the skies where her mother was now eternally safe and blissfully happy.

"I am safe in God now too, Mama," Betteken whispered, looking out the window into the starry heavens. "I hope you know that. No matter where I go here or what I do, I'm safe in God—just like you. I have found a refuge for my soul."

She heard a sound behind her and turned to find Adriaen standing in the doorway. "Are you all right?" he asked softly.

She smiled. "God is on our side, right? There's nothing to fear, even in times of danger and sorrow."

"I am amazed at how peaceful I feel now," he said slowly. "All the suffering we go through is worth it, isn't it? If we're only faithful, we'll see Mama again someday."

Betteken's heart overflowed as she nodded. "I can't wait until that day comes."

Appendix

Maeyken Wens, and some of her fellow-believers, burnt for the testimony of Jesus Christ, at Antwerp, A.D. 1573
(Pages 979–980 in the *Martyrs Mirror*)

The north wind of persecution blew now the longer the more through the garden of the Lord, so that the herbs and trees of the same (that is the true believers) were rooted out of the earth through the violence that came against them. This appeared, among other instances, in the case of a very God-fearing and pious woman, named Maeyken Wens, who was the wife of a faithful minister of the church of God in the city of Antwerp, by the name of Mattheus Wens, by trade a mason. About the month of April, A.D. 1573, she, together with others of her fellow believers, was apprehended at Antwerp, bound, and confined in the severest prison there. In the meantime she was subjected to much conflict and temptation by so-called spirituals (ecclesiastics), as well as by secular persons, to cause her to apostatize from her faith. But when she could by no manner of means, not even by severe tortures, be turned from the steadfastness of her faith, they, on the fifth day of October, 1573, passed sentence upon her, and pronounced it publicly in court at the afore-mentioned place, namely, that she should, with her mouth screwed shut, or her tongue screwed up, be burnt to ashes as a heretic, together with several others, who were also imprisoned and stood in like faith with her.

Thereupon, the following day, the sixth of October, this pious and God-fearing heroine of Jesus Christ, as also her fellow believers that had been condemned with a like sentence, were brought forth, with their tongues screwed fast, as innocent sheep for the slaughter, and each having been fastened to a stake in the marketplace, deprived, by fierce and terrible flames, of their lives and bodies, so that in a short time they were consumed to ashes; which severe punishment of death they steadfastly endured. Hence the Lord shall hereafter change their vile bodies, and fashion them like unto His glorious body. Phil. 3:21.

Further Observation

The oldest son of the aforementioned martyress, named Adriaen Wens, aged about fifteen years, could not stay away from the place of execution on the day on which his dear mother was to be offered up, hence he took his youngest little brother, Hans (or Jan) Mattheus Wens, who was about three years old, upon his arm and went and stood with him somewhere upon a bench, not far from the stakes erected, to behold his mother's death.

But when she was brought forth and placed at the stake, he lost consciousness, fell to the ground, and remained in this condition until his mother and the rest were burnt. Afterwards, when the people had gone away, having regained consciousness, he went to the place where his mother had been burnt, and hunted in the ashes, in which he found the screw with which her tongue had been screwed fast, which he kept in remembrance of her.

There are at present, 1659, several grandchildren (well known to us) still living of this pious martyress, who are named after her.

Author's Postscript

The tongue screw that Adriaen Wens found in the ashes is now preserved in the Mennonite Archives in Amsterdam, the Netherlands.

In 1576, three years after this story takes place, Spanish soldiers ransacked the city of Antwerp, killing thousands of people. Whether the Wens family actually fled the city or not is unknown. But the legacy of their faith lives on, encouraging us to be found among the faithful when God calls us home.

Dutch Pronunciation Key

Adriaen	AH-dree-ahn
Anthonis Ysbaerts	Ahn-TOH-nĭs ICE-bahrts
Betteken	Same as English
Dirk Willems	Dirk VĬL-ehms
Felix Straten	FEE-lĭks STRAH-tehn
Friesland	FREES-lahnd
Ghent	Gehnt
Grietge	KHREET-khuh

This name has no English equivalent for pronunciation. The "KH" is used to represent a sound as if you're clearing your throat, a throaty, rumbly "H." It's similar to the German "CH."

Hans van Muntsdorp	Hahns fahn MĬNTS-dorp
Jan de Metser	Yahn dĭ MEHT-suhr
Janneken	YAHN-eh-kehn
Johannes	Yoh-HAHN-ehs
Joos Marten	YOHS MAHR-tehn
Lijsken	LICE-kehn
Lucia	LOO-see-ah
Maeyken	MAY-kĭn
Margretha	Mahr-GREHT-ah
Mariken	MAHR-ĭ-kehn
Maritgen	MAHR-ĭt-hehn
Mattheus	Maht-TAY-us
Pieter	Peter
sluberkens	sloo-BAIR-kehns
Wens	Vehns
Wils	Vĭls

About the Author

Diane Yoder hones her story-writing craft in southern Indiana, where she lives with her parents and three of her siblings. A longtime lover of writing, Diane published her first story when she was fourteen years old. Through the encouragement of her friends and family, she decided to pursue her dream of writing books. She has written two other books, *Pardon's Price* and *Where the Road Divides*.

Diane is a member of Living Waters Mennonite Church. She delights in the beauty she finds in nature, music, words, and people. Her desire and prayer is that her readers will learn to trust the Saviour and receive His love.

If you wish to contact Diane, you may write to her at 10279 West Polk Road, Lexington, IN 47138, or at Christian Aid Ministries, P.O. Box 360, Berlin, Ohio 44610. She would be happy to hear from you!

Christian Aid Ministries

Christian Aid Ministries was founded in 1981 as a nonprofit, tax-exempt 501(c)(3) organization. Its primary purpose is to provide a trustworthy and efficient channel for Amish, Mennonite, and other conservative Anabaptist groups and individuals to minister to physical and spiritual needs around the world. This is in response to the command ". . . do good unto all men, especially unto them who are of the household of faith" (Galatians 6:10).

Each year, CAM supporters provide approximately 15 million pounds of food, clothing, medicines, seeds, Bibles, Bible story books, and other Christian literature for needy people. Most of the aid goes to orphans and Christian families. Supporters' funds also help clean up and rebuild for natural disaster victims, put up Gospel billboards in the U.S., support several church-planting efforts, operate two medical clinics, and provide resources for needy families to make their own living. CAM's main purposes for providing aid are to help and encourage God's people and bring the Gospel to a lost and dying world.

CAM has staff, warehouse, and distribution networks in Romania, Moldova, Ukraine, Haiti, Nicaragua, Liberia, and Israel. Aside from management, supervisory personnel, and bookkeeping operations, volunteers do most of the work at CAM locations. Each year, volunteers at our warehouses, field bases, DRS projects, and other locations donate over 200,000 hours of work.

CAM's ultimate purpose is to glorify God and help enlarge His kingdom. ". . . whatsoever ye do, do all to the glory of God" (1 Corinthians 10:31).

The Way to God and Peace

We live in a world contaminated by sin. Sin is anything that goes against God's holy standards. When we do not follow the guidelines that God our Creator gave us, we are guilty of sin. Sin separates us from God, the source of life.

Since the time when the first man and woman, Adam and Eve, sinned in the Garden of Eden, sin has been universal. The Bible says that we all have "sinned and come short of the glory of God" (Romans 3:23). It also says that the natural consequence for that sin is eternal death, or punishment in an eternal hell: "Then when lust hath conceived, it bringeth forth sin: and sin, when it is finished, bringeth forth death" (James 1:15).

But we do not have to suffer eternal death in hell. God provided forgiveness for our sins through the death of His only Son, Jesus Christ. Because Jesus was perfect and without sin, He could die in our place. "For God so loved the world that he gave his only begotten Son, that whosoever believeth in him should not perish, but have everlasting life" (John 3:16).

A sacrifice is something given to benefit someone else. It costs the giver greatly. Jesus was God's sacrifice. Jesus' death takes away the penalty of sin for everyone who accepts this sacrifice and truly repents of their sins. To repent of sins means to be truly sorry for and turn away from the things we have done that have violated God's standards (Acts 2:38; 3:19).

Jesus died, but He did not remain dead. After three days, God's Spirit miraculously raised Him to life again. God's Spirit does something similar in us. When we receive Jesus as our sacrifice and repent of our sins, our hearts are changed. We become spiritually alive! We develop new desires and attitudes (2 Corinthians 5:17). We begin to make choices that please God (1 John 3:9). If we do fail and commit sins, we can ask God for forgiveness. "If we confess our sins, he is faithful and just to forgive us our sins, and to cleanse us from all unrighteousness" (1 John 1:9).

Once our hearts have been changed, we want to continue growing spiritually. We will be happy to let Jesus be the Master of our lives and will want to become more like Him. To do this, we must meditate on God's Word and commune with God in prayer. We will testify to others of this change by being baptized and sharing the good news of God's victory over sin and death. Fellowship with a faithful group of believers will strengthen our walk with God (1 John 1:7).